The

DOME-SINGER
of FALENDA

KATHERINE BOLGER HYDE

WAYSTONE
PRESS

Published by Waystone Press
http://www.waystonepress.com

Originally published by Oloris Press 2016

ISBN: 978-1-7320873-2-3

To Jonah

and to the children of St. Lawrence Academy
past, present, and future

CHAPTER ONE

In Which I Lose My Balance

THE DAY FIRST SHIFTED OUT OF KILTER when I had my little chat with the Canon.

We'd finished rehearsal with my favorite high C. I love to listen to it echoing up to the highest arches of the cathedral, to follow the sound out through the stained-glass window and up into the atmosphere, where it shoots like a rocket out beyond the stars. But I always have to come back to Earth eventually. My voice may someday be my ticket out of this life, but for now it's all I've got.

Canon Howard turned his ray-gun glare on us choristers. "Good work, Danny. The rest of you really must tighten your timing, or the Lessons and Carols will be a victory for the Adversary and not a glory to God."

Bull and his toadies shoved past me on the way out of the stalls, making gargoyle faces and mouthing "Good work, Danny." They threw their robes in a heap on the vestry floor and clattered out. I hung about, straightening my robe on the hanger and smoothing the collar.

The Canon came in clucking like a mother hen. "I spend my life's blood trying to make music to glorify God, and what does he send me? A pack of croaking frogs who won't even bother to hang up their robes!" He bent down to pick up Bull's robe, which is about the size of a young dirigible, and saw me behind the rack. "Except for you, Danny. I can forgive God when I remember he sent me you."

I always think the Canon must be talking about someone else when he talks like that, but it feels good all the same. I supposed he wouldn't bite me if I asked him. As for Dad, now, that's another story—if he found out I'd so much as mentioned the subject of money to anyone at the cathedral, he'd go ballistic.

"Canon Howard—" I started, but then my voice broke into a squeak. It's been doing that more and more lately—once or twice even when I was singing, though the Canon hasn't noticed yet. I hoped he'd go on not noticing, because I didn't know what would happen once I lost my treble range.

But the Canon turned those sharp dark eyes my way, and I knew he was onto me. "How old are you, Danny?" he asked with a voice like a knife.

"Fourteen in March, sir."

He scrunched his foxtail eyebrows together until his forehead looked as if someone had gone over it with a lawnmower but missed a strip right along the edge. "I always forget your age, you're so small. We'll be losing you soon. Lucky if you make it to Easter."

"Losing me, sir?" He couldn't mean it had already been decided I'd have to leave the school at the end of the term.

"As a treble, that is. Not altogether. You do plan to stay on for upper school, I hope?"

"Well, sir—I'd like to stay, of course. But—" How could I say it without crossing Dad's invisible line? Invisible, but touchy as an electric fence. "Hypothetically, sir—if a boy wanted to stay on but his family couldn't afford it—"

The corners of the Canon's mouth twitched. "*Hypothetically,* we can always find a scholarship for a talented treble. Or tenor, as the case may be."

"Even—for a boarder, sir?"

One foxtail arched up so it looked as if the man with the lawnmower must have been drunk. "A boarder? Is this hypothetical family thinking of leaving Midchester?"

"Just curious, sir, you know—hypothetically." I couldn't help a little grin. He was onto me, but he wouldn't give me away.

"Then I think that might be hypothetically possible."

I dropped the other shoe. "What if the boy's father didn't want him to come?"

He pierced me with those needle-sharp eyes until I squirmed like a first-year boy desperate for the loo. "Suppose I have a little talk with this hypothetical father? Say this evening?"

"Sir—you won't let him know I said anything, will you? He made me promise not to tell."

"You haven't told me a thing, Danny. Just asked a lot of hypothetical questions." He grinned. "Now you'd better get going, your father will be missing you. I'll be along in a little while."

That's when it happened. He turned to the side and I heard, "God help me wring anything out of that drunken beast."

I stood rooted, the hairs on my arms standing up as if ready to take flight. It wasn't so much what the Canon said that shocked me—that was true enough, though I'd never have thought he'd say it aloud in my presence. What threw me was that *his lips hadn't moved at all.* They were clamped together like a vise.

I ducked out onto the cloister lawn and took a few deep breaths, leaning against the ancient stone wall of the cathedral. The stress must really be getting to me. I was hearing things.

The prospect of leaving the choir school was certainly enough to drive me barmy. Singing is my life. It's the only thing I can do. Forget games—I can't see the point of running around a field after a ball. And forget lessons—I've got music playing in my head round the clock, even in my sleep. Throw in figures and names and dates and it's a jumbled-up mess. If I lost my chance to sing, I'd lose everything.

I walked out a few paces and turned back to look at the cathedral with its spire soaring into the sky. The sight of it always comforts me, like there's one thing in the world that will never go bad on me. When I was small, I was sure the carved saints on the west front were watching me everywhere I went—not scary watching, but looking out for me the way my mum did back then. They had to protect me from the gargoyles, who crouched on the parapets and leered out of the gutter spouts, ready to pounce the minute the saints closed their eyes—which, fortunately, they never did.

Now I whispered up to the saints, "Help me on this one, won't you? Don't let him take me away." I homed in on St. Cecilia, my mother's name saint and the patroness of music. Then I blinked and looked again. I could have sworn I saw her nod.

Barmy for sure.

I turned to go, and there they were—Bull and his toadies, in a semicircle and closing fast. They must have been really brassed off, or really bored, to wait around for me all this time.

I pulled my stomach up off my knees and got into a boxer's stance, ready for any sudden movement. I already knew the theme of their fugue.

Sure enough: "Where's your mum, Danny-boy?" Bull sang out. Creeper took up the counter-melody: "Took her off to the loony bin, they did!" Weasel came in on cue: "Couldn't stand to be around this little prig—threw herself in the ocean!" Then the whole lot of them chanted in unison: "Threw herself in the ocean! Threw herself in the ocean!" as they came for me.

It's always the same. They were lying, of course, but how could I prove it? My mum disappeared when I was six. Just gone. Poof. Not a trace of her. Even my memories of her were unraveling like a worn-out robe. The more I clung to the shreds I had—stargazing on the bell tower, watching butterflies on the cloister lawn, singing Christmas carols together— the faster they disintegrated. I could still hear her singing, though. Everyone says I get my voice from my mum, along with my fair hair.

But my temper comes from my dad.

Here was another thing different about that day. Usually when things get to that point, I run for the bell tower, all the way to the top. I may be small, but I'm fast, and they're too lazy to follow me past the first flight.

But that day I didn't feel like running. I felt like fighting. You ever hear of berserkers? Those old Norse warriors who went crazy on the battlefield and slaughtered everyone for miles around and couldn't be hurt? I felt like one of them. I felt like mutilating the whole gang.

My fists balled up of their own accord and started to rise. And then I heard a voice just behind me.

9

"What's all this? Picking on the smallest boy again? You lot get off home before I call the constable and let him give you what you deserve."

Canon Howard. He must have spoken aloud that time. With a glare that told me next time I'd be like Frodo facing the Black Riders, Bull and his minions scarpered.

The wind went out of me like a balloon. I should have been relieved, since I'm not really a berserker, and the gang would no doubt have clobbered me. But instead I felt oddly let down.

"Since you're still here, Danny, how about me walking you home?"

We crossed the close in silence—me jumpy lest I start hearing things again—then turned down the cobblestone street that leads to my house. When the Canon finally spoke, I kept my eyes on his lips to be sure they were moving.

"It may be my fault those boys pick on you."

"Oh no, sir. I'm an easy target."

"No, it's more than that. They're jealous of you."

It was all I could do not to guffaw at that. Who'd want my life? No mum, no friends, a home I only go to in order to keep out of the rain—and now the barminess.

But the Canon's narrow chin bobbed. "Because of your voice. And because I tend to make a bit of fuss over you. Wrong of me to single anyone out like that, but I've always felt you needed a bit of encouragement."

He got that one right. I certainly didn't get encouragement from anyone else.

"If I treat you—differently—from now on, Danny, don't take it personally. It'll just be my way of evening the playing field." He stopped outside my door and turned me to face him. "You understand?"

I kept my eyes steady on his. "Yes, sir."

He knocked on my front door. After a bit the door opened a crack, and my father's unshaven mug poked out.

"Fine time to show up," Dad growled down at me, then looked past me to the Canon. He widened the crack to the width of his body—a laborer's body gone to flab—and straightened to his full height, which matched the Canon's six-foot-plus. Their height was the only thing they had in common.

"Canon Howard. What's this? Boy been making trouble?"

"Nothing like that, Mr. Cutler. Danny is a fine boy and a superb musician. But I would like to speak to you for a few minutes, if I may."

Dad stood back to let us in. "Go to your room, boy," he said to me, with a shove on the shoulder that could almost have passed for a pat.

I shut my door with an audible click, waited a few seconds, then eased it ajar and stood close behind it. I had to hear them decide my fate.

They kept their voices low, and all I got was a word here and there. Something about "upper school," "scholarship," and "like to keep him" from the Canon, countered by "go where the work is," "no handouts," "boy's got to face facts" from Dad. Then footsteps and the outer door scraping shut.

I heard my father's boots thudding toward my room and shut the door, then leapt onto the bed and grabbed the nearest book. Fortunately I grabbed it the right way up.

He poked his head in. "I'm going out." *Out* meaning down the pub. I cracked his code years ago. "Get those lessons done and get to bed." His head disappeared.

I screwed my courage to the sticking point. "Dad—" His head popped in again, like a jack-in-the-box. "Dad—if they

11

give me a scholarship—couldn't I stay on? as a boarder?"

The veins in his forehead bulged. "You're going to vocational school, learn a real trade. Singing's no job for a man."

I was about to argue further when I heard a faint mumbling: "Just like her . . ."

And his lips hadn't moved either.

He pulled his head back and shut the door. The walls shook as the front door slammed behind him.

If I had to hear people's thoughts, couldn't I hear something pleasant?

Of course I'd known all along on some level: when he looks at me, he's seeing Mum. As long as I'm around, he can never forget.

And singing is what she wanted for me.

I went to the kitchen and opened a few cupboards. A tin of sausage and beans, a pack of pot noodles. A swallow of milk and some wilted lettuce in the fridge.

I wasn't that hungry anyway. This was a bell tower night.

MIDCHESTER IS JUSTIFIABLY PROUD OF its bell tower. As the cathedral guide will tell you, it dates from the fifteenth century and is the only freestanding medieval bell tower in England. As only a handful of locals can tell you, it's a great place to stargaze, watch the sunset, or just be alone for a while. Mum and I used to come up here all the time. Now I come up by myself.

I flattened myself behind a buttress and waited for the old verger to come and unlock the door to ring the bells for Evensong. I slipped in behind him and crouched under the stairs while he wheezed up them, rang the bells, and stumped down again. Then I sprinted to the top of the tower.

Leaning on the parapet to catch my breath, I gazed at the whole town spread out below me. The last red rays of the sun glinted off the tile roofs, turning this ordinary place into fairyland. My favorite time of day. I squinted at the red rim of the sun as it slipped below the horizon, and I could swear a piece of it broke off and flew toward me—a scrap of red, fluttering over the rooftops, making straight for the tower.

At first I thought I was seeing things again. Then I laughed. It was only a butterfly. But a solid red one? I've seen hundreds of species in my time. I've got drawings of them all in my notebook at home, labeled with their proper names, Latin and vernacular. But you hardly ever see a wing pattern that's just one solid color—certainly not tomato red. Mum would have been so excited, she'd have danced right over the parapet.

Mum. The red butterfly swam in my vision, and I put my hand in my pocket for the one thing that can ground me when I get these blitz grief attacks: Mum's music box.

Dad had it made specially for her. It's tiny, the size of my palm, shaped like a Purple Emperor butterfly with the wing pattern inlaid in enamel on the top. When you open it, the inside of the lid holds a picture of the three of us, me just a baby in Mum's arms, and it plays the tune she used to sing me to sleep with: "O Danny Boy."

I opened it and listened to the tune, Mum's voice singing it in my head. "Mum," I whispered, "you've got to help me before I lose it completely. Make Dad let me stay at the choir school. Help him be himself again."

I closed the box and slid it back in my pocket, then blinked the strange butterfly into focus. It was close now, and I could see its wings really were solid red. But—I couldn't see a body between them. And the wings seemed to change shape as it flew.

I leaned over the parapet and stretched out one arm, hoping the butterfly might come to me, but it hovered just out of my reach, teasing me. Or—peculiar thought—beckoning me? I put a knee up on one of the crenellations, balancing with the opposite hand on the top of the parapet, and stretched as far as I could toward it.

Too far. My balance shifted, and I fell.

CHAPTER TWO

In Which I Meet a Very Unusual Girl

Y OU DON'T FALL FROM A HEIGHT like that and not die. Or so I thought.

I must have blacked out before I hit the ground—I don't remember feeling any impact. But then I came to and opened my eyes. Mind you, I assumed I was dead, but for some reason that thought didn't bother me much. Above me was all gold, as if someone had taken the sun and spread it right across the sky. I could look at it without blinking. I guessed that must be the light people talk about when they come back from a near-death experience. Well, death could be better than what I'd left behind. If this was heaven, maybe I'd meet my mother here.

But I wasn't walking into the light; I was lying on the ground. Still inside my body. I wiggled my fingers and toes, flexed my knees. No pain, and everything worked fine. So, not dead? Not even injured? Impossible.

I'd entered the realm of the impossible. That was worse than being dead. Death might be the undiscovered country, but at least my Anglican upbringing had given me some idea what to expect on the other side. This place didn't look like anything that was mentioned in catechism class.

I sat up—slowly, dizzily—and looked around. I was definitely not at the bottom of the bell tower. A meadow, all flat, stretched out far on every side. A meadow full of violets. But wait—not flowers. More like violet-colored grass. Around the edges of the meadow grew some taller, nubbly stuff—I would have said a forest except it was orange. I took a cautious breath. The air smelled like roses mixed with the tang of the sea.

It was beautiful, but it was all wrong. Not one thing was the way it should be. Where in the world was I?

Or—where out of the world? And how had I gotten here?

All the other-world stories I'd ever read sprang up and jostled for space in my mind. My throat went dry. Anything might happen in a place like this. The innocent-looking grass might snake out and wrap itself around my throat. That seeming forest might turn out to be an army of orange giants, to whom a small terrified boy would be a succulent snack.

Then I saw the butterflies. Like the one on the tower, but dozens of them, each a different hue, as if someone had broken a prism and all the colors had come fluttering out. Their wings changed shape as they flew, as if they were made of flickering flame. Not butterflies at all, really, but I had no other name for them.

The big red one from the tower—at least I assumed it was the same one—hovered before my face, so close I could hardly focus on it. I leaned hard on my hands so they wouldn't bat it away.

Then I heard something in my mind—not coming through my ears, just there, in my mind—like an echo inside a cave. It came again, then again, each time more distinct, until it began to sound a bit like speech. I concentrated on it as hard as I could and finally made out the words, or at least the meaning: "Are you all right?"

I took a cautious look round just to be sure. Nope, no one there. Just me and the not-butterflies.

From hearing people's thoughts to telepathy with bodiless wings may not seem like such a stretch. But throw in the whole imagined world, and I must be nutty as a fruitcake.

Or perhaps only dreaming. That was some comfort.

The red wings fluttered back and forth as if the creature were looking into each of my eyes, though it had no eyes that I could see. And the echo-voice came again. "Are you all right?"

My body was all right, even if my mind had gone out to lunch and forgotten to leave a call-back number. I nodded. That was as far as I was willing to go toward conversing with a pair of wings.

The wings fluttered upward as if they wanted me to stand up. Might as well—at least then I'd be ready to run if need be. In dreams I always end up running sooner or later.

The red wings darted ahead a few feet, then back toward me. When I didn't move, the echo-voice said, "Come. There is nothing to fear."

Nothing to fear? My whole world had turned itself inside out, and there was nothing to fear? And besides, this was the creature that had lured me to fall from the tower. Why should I trust it now?

Up to that point, I thought I knew what it was to be alone. But until you've been the only human in a landscape in which not one single thing is familiar, you don't have a clue.

I didn't move, but looked where the not-butterflies were heading. And saw a figure coming toward me across the meadow. An upright figure, apparently more or less human.

This could be good news. Or it could be very bad. The figure was coming straight toward me—no place to run, no place to hide. There *is* something worse than being entirely alone, and that's being alone with a creature that might want to kill you.

The figure was walking fast, almost skimming over the grass. Soon I could see it was wearing a long gown and was shaped like a girl, but the slenderest girl I'd ever seen. Not bony, just incredibly narrow. My jacket would have gone round her twice, and I'm the skinniest kid I know.

One good thing: I couldn't see any weapons. Of course, she might have weapons of a completely different kind.

Her gown was made of some light, iridescent stuff that shimmered into different colors as she walked. At first I thought the gown had lavender sleeves, but a few paces later I realized it was sleeveless—her face and hands were lavender too. Her eyes were golden, with no whites in them, and her hair—

Well, I had to call it hair. But it wasn't really. The strands were all about six inches long, and they stood out straight from her head—not stiff, but waving slightly, though there

wasn't any breeze. And the strands were iridescent, like her gown. That, together with the lavender skin and golden eyes, made a pretty striking picture. But not a human picture at all.

She stopped about three feet away and opened her mouth. Her lips moved, but what I heard was wind chimes, tinkling icicles, the ring of a crystal glass being tapped with a spoon.

I just stared at her. What else could I do?

She looked at me with a little crease between those golden eyes, then I heard an echo in my head again—only this one had overtones of her chiming voice. "How have you escaped from the City? And how is it that you do not understand my speech?"

Where could I even begin with that one? City? Escape? Speech? But at least it didn't sound as if she wanted to kill me.

"I don't know what you're talking about," I said lamely. "I fell—from a tower. And then I was here." I looked around at the violet grass, the orange forest, the golden sky. "Wherever 'here' is. If it's even real."

The girl's frown deepened. The not-butterflies fluttered around her head for a minute, then her face cleared. "I see now. The elúndina* have explained to me." Her eyes shone with what looked like excitement, as far as I could read those peculiar whiteless eyes. "You have come to us from another world."

Another world? My mind flattened out like a piece of Silly Putty, then tried to wrap itself around this new idea. Too far to stretch. The corners poked out and stabbed at me.

But all I said was, "Elúndina?"

Her hair-things waved, then the echo-voice said, "The creatures you think of as butterflies. I do not think you have a word for them in your language. They are something like— messengers, perhaps? Or—angels?" She shrugged. "At any rate, it is they who have brought you here. They do the will of the Great One."

Angels that looked like butterflies and could carry people between worlds? Right, I was really going to swallow that one.

---

* Please see page 191 for a pronunciation guide and glossary to the Falendan language.

But on the other hand, I was here. The place felt more real every minute.

"So where is—here? What is this place?"

Her silvery eyebrows rose. "Why, this is Falenda, of course."

I struck the heel of my hand against my forehead. Of course. Falenda. Everybody knows about Falenda. Right there in the astronomy books, out past the sometime planet Pluto.

"Why do your inner thoughts say one thing and your outer thoughts another?" the echo-voice said. "Do you know of Falenda or not?"

Okay, now that was just too creepy. I had not spoken. Apparently this creature not only could project her thoughts into my mind, but she could read my thoughts as well—including the subconscious ones. I'd had schoolmasters who seemed as if they could read my mind, but now I was up against the real thing. I had no place to hide from this girl. Maybe *that* was her secret weapon.

And I didn't even know her name.

I hoped if I spoke aloud she'd hear only that and not the thoughts underneath. "Where I come from that's called *sarcasm*. It's meant to be—sort of funny."

"I do not see that it is funny. It is more like telling a lie. We True Falendans cannot lie. Our thoughts and our speech are one. Perhaps you are a Flattened One after all?" The crease came between her eyes again. "Surely the elúndina cannot have been mistaken?" I heard in a sort of mental mutter, as if she hadn't really intended me to hear.

Flattened One? The words made my gut go cold, though I didn't know why. "I'm not flat. I'm three-dimensional. See?" I held out my arm and turned it about. Then it occurred to me: maybe they have more than three dimensions here.

20

The elúndina fluttered around her again, and her purple lips curved. "You perceive more than you know." Drat, there she went reading my thoughts again. "But that is not what I meant. It seems almost everyone is Flattened in your world, and thus you are not aware of it."

I pictured all of England crushed paper-thin by a giant pavement-roller. But then it all popped up and reinflated like a character in a cartoon. What could she possibly mean?

"But I am tiring you with so much that is new." She could say that again. Fortunately, she didn't. "Come, I will take you to my grandfather. You may rest a while, and then he will tell you why you have come to us and what you are to do."

CHAPTER THREE

In Which I Walk into Adventure

THE GIRL-CREATURE TURNED AND WALKED back the way she'd come, but I didn't follow. I wasn't sure I wanted to buy into this dream, or adventure, or whatever it was, to the extent of going with her and meeting more of her kind.

But what choice did I have? I pinched, poked, and slapped myself on the off-chance I could wake myself up—but of course nothing happened. If you think about it, how could that work, anyway? If it was only your dream-self being pinched, the real you wouldn't feel the pain.

I looked all around me and saw nothing that looked like a way back home—no mystical doors or ladders to nowhere, no odd shimmering in the air that suggested some magical portal. I asked the nearest elúndina, my old friend the red one, if he could take me home, but he only fluttered as if he were shaking his nonexistent head.

And come to think of it, what was so great about home that I should want to go back?

I could try to survive here on my own, but that thought

was way scarier than the prospect of meeting more Falendans. What would I find to eat or drink, and how would I know it wouldn't poison me? And what if there were animals lurking in that orange forest, flesh-eating ones that came out at night to prowl? The golden sky was already beginning to dim; I assumed it would be night before long. Human—or almost-human—company was beginning to sound pretty good.

Anyway, I'd read enough books to know that when it comes to adventures, the only way out is through.

I took a step after the girl-creature, looking down to be sure of my footing, and saw the violet grass stems move aside to make way for my foot. Truly. They didn't bend under my weight or sway in the breeze; there was no breeze. They moved through the dirt, from the roots, to get out of my way. At the same time I heard a little trilling sound, like someone running a finger over a harp.

I looked up again. By now the girl was maybe fifty meters ahead. "Hey!" I called, then immediately felt foolish, because if she could read my thoughts, what point was there in yelling? But old habits die hard. "Hey, what's-your-name, wait up!"

She stopped and turned back. "My name is Mélikulén-duliminála," the echo-voice said. At least, that's the closest I can get to rendering the bell-like sounds I actually heard in my mind.

"Meliku—what?"

"In your language, I believe that translates to Promised Child of the Crystal. But if the name is difficult for you, you may call me Meli, as my grandfather does for short."

"Meli." It just didn't have the same *ring* when I said it. "I'm Danny."

"Dan-ni," she pronounced aloud. My name spoken by

wind chimes. I laughed for sheer pleasure, and she opened her mouth with a sound like water poured over ice cubes in a crystal glass. At least her teeth were the right color. And that lavender-gold-iridescent combo was growing on me. Once I stopped expecting her to look human, I had a hard time tearing my eyes away.

When we got to the edge of the orange forest, she paused and put up a hand. Her hair-things waved in all directions.

"Are there dangers in the forest? Wild animals and whatnot?"

"Wild animals?" Her hair-things bent toward me like probing fingers. "Oh, I see. In your world you have caused animals to fear you, and so you have to tame them to make them serve you. Here among the True Falendans, all animals are our friends. They serve us, but we also serve them. No, the dangers here are of a different kind. The Enemy has his spies among us, and occasionally someone is captured and taken to the City."

I got that same chill again when she said "the Enemy." As if, whatever it was, it was worse than the most ravening beast. "Who is the Enemy? And what's so bad about going to the City?"

She stopped and stared at me. In the depths of her golden eyes was a flame of some deep emotion—just what, I couldn't be sure. "In the City people are Flattened. It is worse than what you call death."

Well, that would explain the chill—if I'd known about it. Maybe I picked up the fear in Meli's mind.

"But I forget. You do not yet understand. My grandfather will explain it all." She started off again, more quickly now. "We must hurry. We dare not be out after sunset. That is when the Enemy's spies can see most clearly."

We trotted down a rough path through the underbrush. After ten or fifteen minutes we pulled up in a small clearing in front of a steep rock face. Several women—larger versions of Meli, but with blue eyes instead of gold—were shooing children through a cleft in the rock. When they caught sight of me, they stared, their eyes widening and their hair-things doing a frantic dance.

"It is well," Meli's echo-voice said, but I knew she was talking to them, not to me. "He is not a Flattened One. The elúndina brought him to us from another world."

Their hair-things calmed down at that, but their odd whiteless eyes still looked wary. They backed away, and Meli led me past them, through the cleft and into a dark passage. But it wasn't dark for long. Meli's hair-things lit up with a white glow, so they looked like superfine fiber optics.

"How do you do that?" I blurted.

"Do what?"

"Make your hair light up like that."

She laughed that tinkling laugh. "How do you make your eyes adjust to the darkness?"

"I don't. It just happens."

"It is the same with our nousíniki."

"With your—what did you call it?"

"Nousíniki."

"And that means—?"

I felt her rummaging around in my mind—like when the dentist uses his mirror to look at all your teeth, and you suddenly remember you forgot to brush before you came. I knew there was stuff in there I didn't want her to see.

"There is no word in your language," her echo-voice said finally. "It is something like 'that which knows the spirit.' But that is only a portion of the meaning. In your world—"

"I know. In my world we don't have things like that." My world was beginning to look pretty lame compared to Falenda.

The passage ended in a sort of cavern, but it was as unlike my idea of "cavern" as the Falendans' nousíniki was—or were?—unlike hair. An open space the size of a small village spread out all around us. The walls, formed of translucent crystal, sloped up as high as the cathedral spire and met at the top in a dome. The last of the golden sunlight filtered down through the top of the dome and shattered into all the colors of the prism.

Around the sides of the cavern, curtains hung from ropes attached to the crystal walls. They were made of the same iridescent fabric as Meli's gown, only heavier. The women and children we'd seen outside split into family groups and ducked behind the curtains.

"Welcome to Kalotelaméliku," Meli said. "The Great Crystal Village."

She pointed toward the far end of the cavern, to a crystal mound with carved steps leading up it and more curtains on top. "That is my grandfather's dwelling."

"Is he like your chieftain or something?"

"He is our logoságami—our wise one. We have no—chieftain?—only the wise one, who conveys to us the messages of the elúndina."

"But you talked to the elúndina in the meadow. Or at least it seemed that way."

"Of course. I have the Blood. I will be logosagami when my grandfather passes into the sky."

"What about your father? Or mother, whoever has the Blood?"

26

"It was my mother." Her echo-voice went tight. "She is gone. My grandfather will tell you. But first, you must eat and rest."

At the word "eat" I realized I was starving. I'd had nothing all day but a cheese sandwich for lunch, worlds and lifetimes away.

Meli led me across the cavern and up the steps of the mound. When we reached the top, a man came out of the curtains, leaning on a carved orange staff. His golden eyes, lavender skin, and iridescent nousíniki looked just like Meli's, but judging by the way he was bent over, he must have been very old.

I waited, clueless about how to greet an aged logosagami. Whatever I expected, it wasn't what happened.

The old man bowed low, his nousíniki touching the rock. "Hail, Deliverer," his echo-voice said. "You have come to us at last."

CHAPTER FOUR

In Which I Get Even More Confused

NEXT MORNING, I WOKE UP in a room made of curtains to find that my own clothes—school suit, knee socks, brogues—were gone. In their place were a sleeveless tunic of that same iridescent fabric and a pair of rope sandals. I panicked for a second until I saw my pocket-things collected in a small orange-wood bowl.

I counted them over: Swiss Army knife, candle stub, matches, a few pence, a couple of small colored stones, an empty sandwich wrapper, and to my intense relief, the Purple Emperor music box. I'd never have forgiven myself if I'd lost that. I lifted the lid a crack and heard the ting of the opening notes of "Danny Boy."

I washed in a little fountain, dressed in the tunic and sandals, and put my pocket-things in a pouch that hung from the belt. Then I heard a phrase of the tinkling Falendan speech. I pulled back the curtain and there was Meli, holding an orange-wood tray.

"You have slept long, Danny," said her echo-voice. "The others have breakfasted, so I have brought you this."

I took the heavy crystal goblet from the tray and sniffed it. It smelled like the same stuff they'd given me the night before. I drank it in one gulp.

The drink wasn't like anything I'd tasted on Earth. It was sweeter than ripe strawberries, more refreshing than spring water, more satisfying than bacon and eggs. "What is this stuff?"

"It is melikunápitu. It flows out of the crystal. Come, I will show you. My grandfather is holding council now, so you cannot speak with him until later."

I followed Meli through the corridors and out onto the steps that led down to the open courtyard. Falendans bustled everywhere. Women washed garments and hung them on lines to dry; old men carved the orange wood; children ran about between the curtained dwellings. And as they worked or played, every single Falendan sang.

It wasn't like any choir I'd heard on Earth. One person would begin a melody that was like a heightening of their chiming speech. Then another would come in with a line of harmony; then a group would repeat the song from the beginning in a round. The music flowed back and forth, around and about, weaving through the people's tasks and binding them together in one ever-changing, joyful song. The way the song resonated within the high crystal cavern reminded me of the cathedral, but Canon Howard would have exploded with glee at these acoustics. I was pretty near exploding myself. I raised my face to the shimmering ceiling, absorbing the music through my pores.

Meli's thought-voice said, "Why do you not sing along?"

"Me? I don't know how to sing like this. I can only sing the songs I've been taught."

"That does not matter. Sing something you know and see what happens."

Pianissimo, I started my solo from the *Christmas Oratorio*. It sounded okay, surprisingly, so I sang a little louder. Then I heard the others' song adjusting around mine, taking up Bach-like harmonies and blending my voice into the whole. I opened up and sang full voice, eyes closed to focus on the sound, and I felt the way I always feel when the music is close to perfection: like my molecules have dissolved into the stuff of the universe and I'm just one tiny piccolo in the music of the spheres.

Then the song cut off all at once, leaving me, like an idiot, to trail off alone. I opened my eyes and saw a commotion near the entrance to the cavern. Two men were riding in on some sort of animal, one man holding the other across his lap. Several villagers crowded around them, while others stood staring, looking too shocked to speak.

"I must look into this," Meli thought to me. "There is no need for you to come." She set off down the steps and across the square, walking so fast her feet hardly seemed to touch the ground.

But I wasn't about to be left behind. Meli was my lifeline in this strange place.

The villagers stepped aside for Meli. The man straddling the beast was pale, breathing in great gasps. But the other, slumped against his chest, looked like death. His skin was a pasty gray, and his nousíniki lay flat against his head like normal hair. His free arm swung limp at his side. He hardly seemed to be breathing.

"Help me," I heard the first man say in my mind. "My brother—I rescued him from the City—but look at him. I took him to our home village, but they could not help him. They said—your logosagami—"

At this he drooped and his hold on the unconscious man loosened. A tall villager stepped forward and caught the sleeper as he fell.

"Come," Meli said to the rider. "You must rest. We will care for your brother. My grandfather is the greatest healer on Falenda. Do not fear."

Two other men helped the rider off the beast, across the square, and into the logosagami's house. Meli and I followed.

"What happened to that man?" I asked her. "He doesn't even look like a Falendan."

Meli was usually serious, but now she looked graver than ever. "He has been Flattened. Like everyone else in the City. He can no longer speak with his thoughts, or light his own way at night, or even sing. He is outside the Fellowship that binds all True Falendans into one people." She took a juddering breath, and I saw a tear escape from one golden eye. "I spoke hopefully to his brother, but in truth I do not know if even my grandfather can save him."

So that was what it meant to be Flattened. I could see what all the fuss was about. My tongue was itching with questions— how could such a thing happen?—but clearly this was not the time to ask them.

Meli led the way to a large room where half-a-dozen Falendans were scurrying about, their nousíniki agitating as if in a proper Channel gale. At the center of the group, on a cushion, sat the old man who had greeted me the night before. The exhausted rider lay propped up on a larger cushion beside him. I heard a babble of voices in my mind but couldn't make sense of them.

31

The old logosagami raised his hand. "Leave me now, my councilors. Our guest is weary. I would speak with him alone."

The others filtered out. I hovered near the doorway. I didn't think I'd be wanted here, but I didn't know where else to go.

"Come, Danny," the old man thought to me. "What we have to hear and say concerns you most nearly."

Concerned me? My stomach gave a flop. I wanted to be concerned in the life of the village, that incredible singing and the sense of belonging that came with it—not in whatever horrors had reduced that poor man to a vegetable. But I went in and sat on a cushion beside Meli.

Meli poured melikunápitu into a crystal goblet and gave it to the rider. He drank like he'd been lost in the desert, then lay back on the cushions with a sigh.

"I am sorry to keep you from your rest, my friend," the logosagami thought to the man. "But if I am to help your brother, I must know something of your story. You are safe here. This is my granddaughter, Meli, and this young man is Danny." The rider looked at each of us, but when his eyes got to me, they turned wary. "Danny has come to us from another world," the logosagami went on. "He is not Flattened as he appears. He knows thought-speech."

The man's eyes widened. "Then—is he—?"

The old man held up his hand. "We will not speak of that yet. I pray you, my friend, tell us your name and your story."

"My name is Vélimir," he replied silently. "I come from Telarímina, the village of the weavers, on the highlands not far from the City. My brother, Kálimir, lived in Telarímina until about a year ago. He went with others from our village to the City to trade our cloth, but he did not return with them. They

32

told me he had taken off his turban just for an hour, because it had become wet."

Meli drew in a sharp breath at this, and her grandfather frowned. What could be so bad about taking off your turban? I hadn't seen anyone in Kalotelaméliku wearing one.

"When the others tried to bring him home with them," Vélimir went on, "he refused to come. To take him by force would have led to their own arrest. They had to leave him behind."

This was beginning to sound like a dystopian novel. And here I'd been thinking Falenda was a utopia.

"I went to the City the next day to bring Kálimir home. But I could not find him, and of course I could not stay more than one night without risk of being Flattened myself. I went back as often as I dared, but it was six months before I found him. By then he was registered as a Citizen and was not allowed to leave. Six more months went by before I could devise a successful plan to rescue him. And by then—" Vélimir buried his face in his hands.

The old logosagami lifted his gnarled hand to Vélimir's shoulder. "And what of your journey?"

Vélimir collected himself. "I took him to our village first, hidden under a load of goods in a cart. While we remained in the City he was healthy enough, although Flattened. But when he came out of the cart into the light and the air, he went into a kind of fit. He danced about, covering first his eyes, then his ears, shaking his head and gasping for breath. Within minutes he became as you saw him. Our healer could do nothing for him, so I brought him to you. He has never revived." Vélimir looked up at the logosagami as a drowning man looks at his rescuer. "Can you help him?"

At that point I realized I was holding my breath. If there was hope for Vélimir's brother to get un-Flattened, there might be hope for this world to become as idyllic as I longed for it to be.

The logosagami lifted his hand, palm outward, and Velimir put his palm up against it. "I will do all that I can for him, I give you my word. But my skill has never yet been tried in a case like this. I cannot promise that I will succeed."

Vélimir's face shrank in on itself, but he nodded and dropped his hand. "Thank you, Logosagami. I will wait and hope."

The old man stood, and Meli and I rose too. "I must go to Kálimir at once. Vélimir, come with me, and I will show you where you may rest."

I turned to Meli with a mind so full of questions they jostled each other in the queue to get out. "What was all that about? What's so important about a turban? How do people get Flattened, anyway? And what's the City got to do with it?"

Meli held up a hand and her face froze in a listening look. Then she thought to me, "My grandfather instructs me to answer your questions, as he is busy with Kálimir. And he has need of more panteléia, a herb that grows in the clearing. Come, we will gather it and I will tell you as we go."

Fine by me. I was way too strung up to sit around at this point.

We started out through the village. Meli was doing that speed-walking thing again. I had to jog to keep up with her. "The City is built over a great lenafálina mine," she began. "The miners—"

"Wait. What's lenafálina?"

Her eyes widened. "Forgive me. I forget how little you know of our world. Lenafálina are like crystals, but they are of many

34

colors, and each color has a special power—some for healing, some for skill in music and poetry and the crafting of beautiful things. The lenafálina are given us by the Great One to be shared freely among all Falendans. But the miners became greedy, wanting more lenafálina to sell to the foreigners from the other side of Falenda, who value them only for their beauty. In their greed, the miners dug too deep, and they opened a rift that led to the prison of Hakagrug, deep in the roots of the mountains."

"What's Hakagrug?" I asked as we came out into the clearing.

"Say rather 'who.'" She paused, looking about, then made for a patch of blood-red ferny things growing up against the rock face a few meters away. I followed.

"Hakagrug is an evil spirit-being of great power, imprisoned beneath the mountains by the Great One in the days when Falenda was young. For thousands of years he slept there, until the miners opened the rift. Then he awoke and began to send his thought-tentacles up to the surface, infecting the minds of the people there. He impelled them to build the City and a great Dome over it. The Dome amplified his power so that he was able to take over the minds of the people completely."

She knelt by the ferns and cupped her hands around one of them, murmuring to it in a voice like a mountain stream. As I watched, it fell over into her palms, its roots dangling out of the soil. That threw me so I almost forgot my question. Oh yeah—took over their minds?

"You mean he sort of hypnotized them?"

She stood and tucked the fern carefully into her belt-pouch, then turned back toward the rock-cleft. "In a sense. He fills their minds with meaningless noise, day and night, so that soon their nousíniki cease to function and lie down flat on their heads. Then they can think of nothing but what Hakagrug implants in their minds. He feeds on their greed and makes them dig faster and deeper, until the day comes when the barriers that confine him will be completely destroyed. Then he will arise and conquer all of Falenda."

We came out of the tunnel into the open courtyard of the village, and I saw her lavender skin was pale. "His power is growing. We are beginning to feel it even here. The day of his triumph will come soon, unless we can break the power of the Dome."

She stopped and looked at me so intently that I had to ask. "We? You mean—does that include me?"

"Why yes, Danny. That is why you were brought here. Did you not know?"

A giant hand reached into my guts and twisted them. "Know what?"

"You are our Deliverer."

That word again. I tried to speak lightly, but that giant hand had grabbed my larynx. "And what's that when it's at home?"

"It is you who must destroy the Dome and set our people free."

Now the giant hand was squeezing my lungs. I gasped for air. "What—me? You're having me on. I'm no deliverer. I'm not brave, or strong, or clever. All I know how to do is sing."

"But singing is precisely what is required. That is how we will break the Dome—by singing. The elúndina chose you for your gifts of singing and thought-speech. And also, of course, because you are your mother's son."

This time the hand got my heart, clenching it so tight it couldn't even beat. "My mother! What's she got to do with it?"

"Did you not know?" she thought again, as if I were a first-former who'd never seen the letter "A." "Your mother was brought here seven years ago to attempt the same task."

Meli hurried on toward the mound where her grandfather's dwelling stood. I forced my legs to follow her, though they were now held in that giant grip.

"Sadly, she failed, and now she is a prisoner in the City. You were brought here not only to save Falenda. You must save your mother as well."

CHAPTER FIVE

In Which I Make a Decision

I RAN UP THE STEPS OF THE MOUND, blood booming like an orchestra of kettle drums in my ears. No way was I taking Meli's word for this. Never mind all that about True Falendans not being able to lie. Surely they could be mistaken. I wanted to hear this from a more reliable source.

I probably would have got myself lost in the corridors in two seconds flat, but I bumped into the logosagami around the first corner. "Sir—what Meli's saying—it can't be true! My mother—in the City?"

The old man looked into my eyes, and I felt as though a cool hand had been laid on my pounding heart. "Let us go to the council chamber," he thought to me. "I am an old man, and this morning has taxed my strength. I must sit."

Sitting was the last thing I wanted to do, but you didn't argue with the logosagami. I followed him. Meli handed the panteléia ferns off to someone and came after us.

When we were seated, the old man turned to me. "It is true,

Danny. To the best of our knowledge, your mother is indeed trapped in the City."

I stared from him to Meli and back again, desperate for some way out. But their minds made a solid wall. "But—that's impossible!"

"Why should it be impossible? You are in Falenda. Your mother disappeared from your world years ago. Why should she not be here too?"

I jumped up in spite of myself. "But why? Why did you take her away from me?" All the sleepless nights with no one to sing to me. All the butterflies I discovered and had no one to share them with. All the solos I'd sung with no friendly face in the audience. And worst of all, the years of watching the father I loved fade away and be replaced by a gruff, unreachable stranger. All of that I'd endured for nothing—so my mother could fail at a task set by aliens.

"The elúndina brought her for the same reason they brought you: she was a singer who had not been fully Flattened. She accepted the quest, and Meli's parents accompanied her. But they were not successful. They were trapped in the City. None of them ever returned." The logosagami's thought-voice tolled like a funeral bell on these words.

I paced in a tight circle, shaking my fists at the air. "First you steal my mother, and now you want me to try something she couldn't do, even with help! You're mental!"

The old man gazed at me. I could tell he felt sorry for me, but not sorry about what he was asking. "It is difficult for you, I know. Please understand that none of this is my decision. I am only an instrument of the Great One's Will. It was he who instructed the elúndina to bring your mother here, and now

39

you. His ways are often inscrutable, but always good. He would not sacrifice you, or your mother, for our deliverance without your willing consent." His nousíniki waved toward me. "And Danny, you will not be alone. You must have a logosagami with you to have any hope of success. Meli has volunteered to go along."

I glanced at Meli and sensed a grief as deep as my own. "Please, Danny." Her thought-voice clanged like a fire bell. "Please help me save our mothers—and our world."

Two children against a formless evil capable of destroying an entire world. It was madness. Of course, it happens in stories all the time. But this was the real world. Some kind of real world, anyway, if not mine.

Meli's ache for her own mother was seeping into my mind, picking at the lock of a door I didn't dare open—I would become a blubbering tot again in no time. But what if it was all a huge mistake? The old man had admitted he didn't know for sure my mother was imprisoned in the City. Maybe she was dead. Maybe—no, she would never have stayed there of her own accord, leaving me orphaned. Would she?

She'd been gone so long. How could I know what she would or wouldn't do? And that creature, Hakagrug, could have done to her what he did to Vélimir's brother. In that case, she might be better off left where she was.

The logosagami's voice answered my thoughts. Was there no privacy with these people?

"Your mother loved you very much, Danny. You may be certain she would not have left you of her own will. She agreed to our request only because we assured her the elúndina could return her to the very moment she disappeared from Earth. And so they would have done, had she not been captured."

40

Well, that was something.

"And I do know that she is alive. When anyone in Falenda dies, that death is felt by all. On the other hand, if she were not trapped in the City, where the elúndina cannot penetrate, they would surely have helped her to return to us. So you see, we have good reason to believe she is imprisoned there. It is not merely what you would call a guess."

I slumped to a cushion, clutching my reeling head. My mum, missing me as she did, had found these people worth risking her life for. She'd always called me her "little knight" when I played at rescuing her from the mop-dragon. She'd be disappointed in me if I refused, even if it were only a question of helping the Falendans. If it was really a matter of rescuing *her*—it might be impossible, but if there was any chance at all, how could I not try?

Then there was Meli. She looked nothing like my concept of a damsel in distress, but she was relying on me. With those golden eyes fixed on me, I couldn't let her down.

I raised my palms and let them drop. "When do we start?"

Meli gave a chiming cry and clapped her hands. Perhaps I could be a knight in shining armor after all.

The logosagami answered, "You must start as soon as possible. The song must be sung at Moon Merge, when the two moons of Falenda cross in their orbits and become one. The pull of the moons from the outside will combine with the force of your song from the inside to shatter the Dome."

Two moons. Okay, I'd seen stranger things. "So, does that happen once a month?"

For the first time the old man's features registered surprise. "Once a month! No, indeed, Danny. The Moon Merge comes but once in every seven years. And then it lasts only moments.

41

It will happen seven days from today."

Seven days! Not much time to go from zero to hero. "How long does it take to get there?"

"Two and a half days to the base of the mountains. A day to climb to the highlands, and a day to cross to the City. Then you will need time in the City to gather other singers to yourselves, for we believe there are some there who are not yet completely Flattened. The more singers you have, the better your chance of success. There is not an hour to lose."

"Come," Meli thought, her golden eyes shining. She rose and held out her hand to me. "We must prepare."

CHAPTER SIX

In Which I Make a Fool of Myself

W E WENT BACK TO THE COURTYARD. The communal song that seemed to go on forever tapered off when we came out. Instead my head filled with dozens of echo-voices, but I couldn't make out what any of them were saying. Meli and I just stood there, and pretty soon people started bringing stuff to us.

Meli bowed her thanks to each person as the pile grew. First came thick cloaks of the same iridescent fabric they seemed to use for everything, which we could also use for blankets. Then there were walking staves of the orange wood, plus collapsible poles, ropes, and more fabric to make a tent. A woman brought large flasks of melikunápitu, the crystal liquid, along with packets of hard cheese and dried fruit.

Each of us got a triangular-bladed crystal knife, the size of my pocket-knife, which we stowed in our belt-pouches. That was the closest thing I saw to a weapon. A sword might have come in handy, but I'd seen nothing made of metal here. Perhaps I could use a tent pole as a quarterstaff—not that I'd have the least idea what to do with it.

And finally, a young chap came in from the clearing with two large animals like the one Velimir had ridden in on earlier.

In size they were somewhere between a donkey and a horse. They had rough smoke-blue coats and grey manes and tails, thick and curly like sheep's wool. Their long heads and splayed feet reminded me of camels', but each had one long twisting horn on its forehead. The closest I'd ever come to seeing a unicorn.

The young chap handed the reins of the smaller one to Meli, and his echo-voice said, "This is Níla." Then he held out the other one's reins to me: "This is Váli."

They expected me to ride this thing. I'd never ridden any sort of animal in my life.

Vali gazed at me with his big, liquid brown eyes, then lowered his horn toward me.

I jumped back, but Meli said, "Do not fear. The balikúni will not hurt you. He wants you to scratch at the base of his horn."

I edged around to Vali's side and put out a cautious hand to rub his smoke-blue fur where it tufted around the base of his silver horn. He made a soft sound between a whicker and a purr and rubbed the side of his head against my chest. Just like a cat. What an idiot I was to be afraid.

"We will ride the balikuni as far as the base of the mountains," Meli said. "After that we will have to go on foot. Their feet are not made for climbing."

What about *my* feet? I'd never climbed a mountain in my life.

Again Meli answered the thought I hadn't spoken. "On this journey I think you will do many things you have never done. But do not worry. Your strength will increase to meet the tasks as they come. Now you must learn to ride."

She sounded like one of the schoolmasters. She couldn't be much older than me, unless they counted time a lot differently here, but she was treating me the way the sixth-formers treat the first-formers at school. I took a deep breath to calm myself, knowing she'd sense my irritation even if I didn't put it into words, spoken or thought. I'd have to find some way of guarding my thoughts from her, or I'd go mad.

Meli moved to Nila's left side, grabbed her woolly mane in her left hand, and in one smooth motion vaulted onto her back. I just stared.

"Come, mount your balikuni."

I would've loved to be able to vault up like that and show her I wasn't a total incompetent. But I knew it was hopeless. Vali's back was level with my armpits. "Look, I've never done this before. No saddle, no stirrups, and you want me to just get on?"

"I do not know these things of which you speak. How else may one mount except by 'just getting on'?"

Clearly I was on my own. I filled my lungs and tightened my abs as I would to sing a high note—like that would help, but it was all I knew. *I can do this.* I took a clump of woolly mane in my left hand, rested my right against Vali's flank, closed my eyes, and jumped.

And landed exactly where I'd started from.

Meli's tinkling laugh rang out, reverberating off the crystal walls until I felt like the whole village—no, the whole *planet*—was laughing at me. "Open your eyes, Danny. You must jump with your legs and push with your arms, and at the same time you must swing your leg over his back."

Why couldn't this be one of those planets with lower gravity?

I took a new grip, bent my knees, pushed hard on Vali's back, and propelled myself upward, remembering at the last minute to swing my right leg up and out.

This time I landed sprawled across his back with my knee barely reaching his flank. Vali turned his head and gazed at me. I slid off again.

Great, I thought. *How am I going to deliver the City if I can't even mount the stupid horse?*

Vali honked like a goose and tossed his horn. Meli said, "You will get nowhere by insulting your mount. It is not his fault you do not know how to ride him."

Blast, there she went invading my mind again. And that wasn't the worst of it. "You mean even the animals around here can read thoughts?"

"Of course. They do not have language, but they understand what relates to themselves."

Of course. I turned to meet Vali's eyes. *I'm sorry I called you a stupid horse,* I thought to him. Somehow thought-speech seemed less scary with an animal. *I'm the one who's stupid. You're a fine and no doubt very intelligent balikuni. But I'm having a little trouble here. Is there any way you can help me?*

Vali dipped his horn as if to say yes, then lowered himself on his front knees. I swung my leg over his back, hung onto his woolly mane with both hands, and he rose to his feet again. I patted his neck and stretched up to scratch around his horn.

Thank you, I thought to him. *I'll get this right eventually.* Vali nodded his horn in agreement.

But Meli looked down her nose at me. "That is the way a child mounts."

That was when I hit my limit. "Well, I am a child! Even in my own world I'm only half grown up. In your world I might as well be a newborn baby for all I know about how things work. Give me a break, can't you? I'm doing the best I can."

Meli's cheeks turned a deep purple and she dropped her eyes. "I have done misamárila. Please forgive me."

Meli embarrassed? You could have knocked me off Vali's back with a swish of a balikuni tail. "Misamárila? What's that?"

"It means a thought or action unworthy of a True Falendan. Something that hurts another and degrades oneself." Her nousíniki waved toward me. "In your language . . . perhaps 'offense'? Or no . . . I think the closest word is 'sin.'"

"I thought—I mean it sounded from what you told me like only the Flattened Ones could sin."

She shook her head. "In the long-ago time, before the foreigners came to the high plains and tempted the miners to dig greedily, there was no misamárila among us. But now that Hakagrug is awake, his evil spreads like a mist over all the land. Even we True Falendans must be watchful that his thought-tentacles do not gain admittance to our minds."

Wow. I'd thought Meli and her people were incorruptible. This mission was even more urgent than I'd known. "We'd better get this riding lesson started."

We walked the beasts around the courtyard while I got used to the balikuni's rolling gait and the feel of his back beneath me. Riding reminded me a little of being on a boat. Keeping myself steady was a challenge, but at least I didn't have to worry about controlling Vali; all I had to do was think what I wanted him to do, and he did it. Once or twice I lost my balance and began to slip to one side, but Vali always shifted to help me right myself.

I began to think I wasn't doing so badly after all. But at

once I sensed a stifled snort of derision from Meli. Okay, so I probably had a long way to go; but couldn't she stay out of my mind in the process?

After half an hour or so, Meli thought to me, "That will have to do for practice. See, our saddlebags are packed and ready. It is time for us to go."

"What, already?"

"You said yourself we had no time to lose."

True, but I'd expected a little more time to prepare myself—a bit of solitude, maybe, in which I could think my own thoughts, steel myself for the coming ordeal. Oh, well, maybe it was better this way. No time to think about all the possible dangers ahead—or my own hopelessness.

I followed Meli to the steps of the mound, watched her Olympic-gymnast-worthy dismount, then slid haphazardly off Vali's back to land on my bum on the rock floor. I could see she was trying hard not to laugh as she helped me to my feet. I swayed a little, like a sailor who hadn't got his land legs back.

We watched as several others loaded Vali and Nila with all the supplies the people had collected. When they finished, I knew I was doomed. Packed saddlebags hung over each bali-kuni's flanks, with another thick bundle balanced between them. Only a narrow strip of Vali's back had been left free for me to sit. If I had trouble mounting before, how could I possibly manage it now? I kept my eyes off Meli, as if that would keep her from sensing how I felt.

But this time, I needn't have worried. Two helpers brought orangewood boxes and set them at the balikuni's left sides. From the box I scrambled onto Vali's back with nothing like grace, but at least with my dignity intact.

Meli mounted as gracefully as always, then smiled at me.

"Only a very tall and strong adult could mount a fully loaded balikuni without a block. You see, we do not expect the impossible."

I managed a tiny smile in return, then we both turned our balikuni to face the courtyard. While we were getting ready, the whole village had gathered in the square. Two women came forward with crystal goblets and offered them to us. I poured the melikunápitu down my throat and felt like my body, at least, was ready for anything.

Then the old logosagami spoke aloud from the steps behind us. Either I was getting used to Falendan communication or they helped me somehow, because I could hear the sense of the words echoed in my mind.

"My people, this is a solemn day in our history. We rejoice this day because the Great One has sent to us a Deliverer from another world. But we send forth our Deliverer—along with our own Mélikulénduliminála—to an uncertain fate. We must pray—now and all the time they are gone from us—that the Great One will grant them victory over the evil that threatens our world. My people, let us pray."

I expected a spoken prayer such as the canon or the bishop might say. But instead they all began to sing. As I listened, I could almost believe there was a Great One guiding all that was happening to me—and that he was expecting me to come up to scratch. As the prayer-song swelled to its finish, I felt my first tiny seed of hope that our quest might be successful.

"Great One," I whispered under my breath, "give me strength."

CHAPTER SEVEN

In Which I Teach Meli a Lesson

W E RODE PAST THE ROWS of Falendans. Each of them held up a hand in salute. It took forever to get through the square and out into the clearing. I gulped the golden air, glad to be away from all those faces—faces full of trust I knew I could never justify. And many of them, the young men's especially, full of the longing to be in my shoes—or sandals, rather. I would've traded places with any of them in the flick of an elúndina's wings.

"Why didn't we bring more people?" I asked Meli. "Plenty of them would've loved to come."

"A large group would attract too much attention. We must go quickly and quietly to avoid detection. Your cloak is on the top of the bundle behind you. Put it on now, before we enter the forest. And from now on, if you wish to speak to me, speak with your thoughts. The balikuni know how to tread silently and how to avoid being seen."

I fumbled behind me and pulled out a large folded lump of the rainbow fabric. I shook it open and threw it over my shoulders, expecting to swelter in the midday warmth. But the cloak was surprisingly light.

"What—" I started to say aloud, then remembered. "What exactly are we hiding from?" I thought it in a mental whisper before I realized how silly that was.

"The Enemy's spies. The níkhi."

Okay. "What's a nikhi?"

"They are the opposite of the elúndina."

Opposite of small bits of flitting color—something huge, grey, and slithery? "Opposite of the elúndina? How?"

"The nikhi are creatures of darkness as the elúndina are creatures of light. That is why they stay mostly in the forest, hidden in the shadows of the malacána trees. And that is why they are most dangerous at night. We will ride through the forest only as far as the meadow where I met you, then keep to the open as much as we can."

That was all she would, or could, tell me, but it didn't explain much. I couldn't blame her. Have you ever tried to describe light to a blind person? If I'd had to explain Earth stuff to her, I couldn't have done any better.

So all I really knew about the nikhi was that we had to hide from them in plain sight. That felt about as comfortable as strolling nonchalantly across the cathedral lawn when I knew Bull and his toadies were lurking in some alley, ready to pounce.

As we moved into the orange forest, I saw what Meli meant about the balikuni's talent for camouflage. A few paces in, the smoke-blue of Vali's coat melted into the same orange as the trees. His mane and tail stayed grey, but since thick grey vines hung everywhere, they blended in too. (Good thing nikhi weren't huge, grey, and slithery—they'd have had the perfect hiding place.) Meli's cloak had lost most of its rainbow and reflected only orange and grey as well. I looked down and couldn't tell where my own cloak ended and Vali's coat began.

I peered about in the gloom for nikhi, all my senses strained until the soft pad of Vali's splayed feet on the forest floor hit my ears like the beating of drums. Then from the corner of my eye I saw, or thought I saw, a kind of flickering darkness in the shadow under a malacána tree. But when I looked straight at it, I saw only solid shadow. I aimed a thought toward Meli: "Was that a nikhi there under that tree?"

Her nousiniki waved toward the tree. "I do not think so. But it is difficult to be sure."

"What happens if they see us?"

"They will follow us, and if they see that we are going toward the City, they will tell their master, Hakagrug. If you begin to feel discouraged, or angry, or fearful, or resentful, that is a sign that nikhi are near. They will do everything in their power to make us turn back."

I'd already felt angry, discouraged, fearful, and resentful even in the supposed safety of the village. Did that make me a nikhi-carrier or something? Or maybe what I'd felt so far was just a little teaser for the big nikhi show. Right now I felt like all they'd have to do to make me turn back was to jump out from the trees and say "boo."

I glanced at Meli, but she seemed lost in her own thoughts, for once not eavesdropping on mine. To distract myself from nikhi-paranoia, I let down my guard and thought about Meli herself. Her faintly glowing nousíniki above the orange of her cloak made an eerily beautiful picture, like a floating ball of pixie light. What could I ever hope to have in common with someone like her? And why did I care?

At last we came out into the meadow, a rippling sea of violet grass. Each stem seemed to strain upwards to meet the golden light, which poured its warmth over everything like a caress. No shadows here—no place for nikhi to hide. The balikuni's coats turned violet, and our cloaks melted into the sky. I took a long breath and turned my face up to the light.

The meadow stretched clear to the horizon. Meli looked at me, and I saw trouble in her golden eyes. Not nikhi trouble—girl trouble.

"Here we have open space enough to move more quickly," she thought to me. "It is time you learned to trot."

I was feeling pretty good about my riding at that point, and I knew Vali would help me out if I needed it. How hard could it be?

Nila broke into a slow trot, and Vali followed suit. At the first step, my confidence flew into the air along with my bum and didn't come back. But my bum came down with a thud. Vali's back was a lot harder than it looked.

Meli was unfazed. "You must rise a little in your seat when the balikuni's back goes down, then gently lower yourself to meet it when it rises again. Like this." She rode a little ahead, gracefully rising and falling with each pace of Nila's trot. All she needed was some jodhpurs and a helmet, and she'd be one of those toffs in the steeplechase I'd seen on the telly back home.

"How in the world do you do that without stirrups to push off from?"

"Hold on with your knees. Not too tightly, or you will hurt your mount."

Right. I'd hurt my mount. Of course it didn't matter if I hurt my *me*.

But Vali was a good balikuni, and I didn't want to hurt him if I could help it. *Here goes nothing,* I thought to him as I tightened my knees to his flanks.

I pushed off from my knees, then relaxed, only to crash like a sour note. The next rise caught me before I could brace myself and sent me flying—this time clear off the balikuni. I landed on my back in the violet grass, gasping for breath.

Then Meli's face was hovering over mine. I read concern in her eyes, but a smirk lurked in the corners of her mouth. "Are you all right?"

No, I'm not all right, you precious purple princess, I thought in spite of myself. I struggled to my feet, ignoring her outstretched hand. *I'm battered and bruised and I think my tailbone is broken, and you're laughing at me.*

Aloud I grumbled, "I'm all right," dusted myself off, then looked up at her face.

Her eyes were wide and flashing, her lips in a thin line. "How dare you speak to me like that! I am a logosagami!"

I was sorry—for about a nanosecond. How dare *I*—? "I wasn't speaking to you! Where I come from, there is such a thing as a private thought. We have a saying: People who eavesdrop hear no good of themselves. If you'd stop eavesdropping in my head, maybe you wouldn't hear the uncomfortable truths your own people are too polite to tell you!"

I whirled away from her and stalked back to Vali's left side. Vali nudged me apologetically.

It's not your fault, mate, I thought to him. *I haven't got a mounting block. Can you kneel down for me?*

Vali knelt, and I clambered onto his back, wincing as my tailbone touched down. Then I turned to Meli.

She hadn't moved. She was staring at me with eyes that

reminded me of the way I felt after one of Dad's tongue-lashings. Suddenly I felt a right git.

"Look, Meli, I'm sorry. It's just—I'm having a really hard time with all this. It did look like you were laughing at me. I'll say pax if you will."

She shook her head. "No. The fault is mine. I was wrong to laugh at you, even on the inside. And I was wrong to—what did you call it—eavesdrop on your thoughts. Among my own people, it is always clear which thoughts are public and which are not. But your mind has no barriers. I yielded to the temptation to come and go there at will." She hung her head, hands limp at her sides. "I have done misamárila again. Please forgive me."

I felt the blood rising to the roots of my hair. She might have been in the wrong, but for her to humble herself before me was like the queen bowing to her bootblack. "Hey, it's okay. I overreacted. Pax?" I put my right hand out toward her.

She stared at my hand. "What is this—pax? And what am I to do with your hand?"

"Pax means peace. We start over with a clean slate, friends. And you're supposed to put your hand in mine and shake it. It's what we do when we make an agreement."

"I see." She looked at me doubtfully, but put her left hand in mine and waggled it.

I laughed. "No, your right hand." She blushed purple, whisked her left hand away and held up her right. I gave it one brisk shake. "That's more like it."

She dropped her eyes and her hand and stepped to Nila's side. I was pleasantly surprised to see Nila drop to her knees for Meli to mount.

Meli turned to face me again. "If you are not too much injured, do you wish to try trotting again?"

That was the first time she'd asked me what I'd like to do instead of telling me. "Sure, I'll give it another shot. What did I do wrong before?"

"You rose at the wrong time. And even when you lower yourself, you must not relax. Trotting requires constant control."

I took a deep breath and mentally signaled Vali to start trotting. When his back fell under me, I lifted from my knees, then lowered myself just slightly to meet his back as it rose with the next pace. Vali purred encouragement, and Meli nodded. "That is better." My bum agreed.

We trotted for a few minutes, then just as I was getting the hang of it, Meli thought, "That is enough for now. It is tiring to trot until your muscles are accustomed to it. And we do not need the speed at this time. It is not far to the village where we must sleep this night."

I nodded, hoping she wouldn't notice how relieved I was. My muscles were screaming already; I couldn't have kept it up if she'd dared me.

We skirted the edge of the trees for a couple more hours at a walk. The gold of the sky began to fade, and our shadows stretched out long beside us. Meli thought to me, "Here we must enter the forest again. The village is within the trees. We must be wary, for the shadows grow deep. Do not speak to me, even in your thoughts, and try to make your mind as blank as you can."

CHAPTER EIGHT

In Which I Climb a Tree
and Meet a Bridegroom

I'D BEEN THINKING OF NOTHING in particular, but as soon as I tried to wipe my mind clear of thoughts, it filled with a whole crowd of questions. Where were we going? Would this village be like Meli's, or something completely different? Were there really nikhi hiding in the shadows? Would I know if they saw me? Maybe I could fight them off and impress Meli. How did one fight nikhi, anyhow?

This wouldn't do. I shook my head and tried to focus on my surroundings. I peered at the rough, ridged texture of the malacána bark, listened to the clear, musical cry of a bird, inhaled the sharp, fresh smell of the trees, like cedar mixed with peppermint and cinnamon. I felt the chafing of Vali's thick, soft coat beneath my legs, the still, cooling air against my cheeks.

When was the last time I'd stopped to pay attention to things like that? At home I was either buried in memories or planning how to cope with the next calamity. I'd forgotten how to just *be*.

Meli stopped and motioned for me to draw Vali up beside her. Before us was a large clearing. In the center of it hung what looked like a vast, circular blue curtain, a hundred feet or more across.

Meli called out something in her chiming voice. The curtain parted and a tall man stood in the gap.

The man returned Meli's spoken greeting, then I heard an anxious voice in my mind: "Who is that with you?"

Meli's thought-voice said, "I bring you our Deliverer, sent to us by the Great One in the hour of our need. We go to the City for Moon Merge."

The man's voice grew more agitated. "He looks like a Flattened One."

"That is because he comes from another world. Most of the people there are Flattened, but Danny understands thought-speech. He is the son of Celia, who was sent to us before."

We'd been walking the balikuni into the clearing as they spoke. Now I could see the blue circle was not a curtain, but a tangle of vines, so dense it seemed like a solid mass. All the vines hung from the branches of a single enormous tree.

I could also see the face of the man who'd greeted us. He was young, only a few years older than me, and his brows were drawn down over blue eyes. Not a logosagami, then. I'd figured out somewhere along the way that all logosagamis had golden eyes.

"Why should he do better than his mother did? How can two children succeed where three adults failed?"

Good question. I would've liked an answer to that one myself. But Meli drew herself up, and I was glad the fire of her golden eyes, for once, was not directed at me. "We may be children, but we do the will of the Great One. It is not by our own strength that we hope to succeed, but by his."

The vines drew back farther, and a golden-eyed woman appeared. "What is it, Lódamor?" Her thought-voice rang like the higher-toned cathedral bells.

"Meli is here. She claims this boy is our Deliverer."

The woman turned to me with a smile. Her nousíniki waved toward me, then she raised her hand, palm outward. "Hail, Deliverer!"

I wished they'd cut the deliverer stuff. "Please, call me Danny."

"You are most welcome to our village, Danny. I am Nitána, logosagami of Telatilamélu, the Village within the Vines. This is my son, Lódamor. Please, come into shelter."

Lodamor took his mother's arm and turned her toward him, frowning into her face. I couldn't hear what they said to each other—I suppose they were talking on a private line— but it didn't seem to lead to any resolution. Lodamor was still sending out very unfriendly vibes as he pulled the vine-curtain wider and stood aside for us to ride through.

At Nitána's call, a second man appeared. Lodamor knelt next to Nila. Meli put her foot on his knee and used his support to make a graceful dismount. The new chap knelt by Vali, and I tried to follow suit, but my leg was too stiff to clear the bundle between my saddlebags. Straining to swing it over, I lost my grip on Vali's mane, flailed helplessly for a second, and fell in a heap of useless limbs onto the fellow's lap. At least Meli wasn't watching. The fellow helped me to my feet without so much as a chuckle.

I thanked him and stood as tall as I could, grasping for one last shred of dignity. But with the first step my knees buckled under me. I had to grab Vali's mane for support. He nudged me with a sympathetic honk. Every muscle in my body ached, including ones I didn't know I had.

Nitana led the way to a ladder of boards fastened to the tree trunk. Meli climbed up, and I struggled after her.

About seven feet above the ground, the branches began, and we were surrounded by orange foliage. A few steps more. and we came up through a hole into a clear space.

I stepped off the ladder onto a broad platform made of narrow interwoven branches that spanned half a dozen sturdy boughs. I could glimpse at least a dozen other ladders and platforms off to the sides, and more levels above. This was a treehouse to rival Lothlórien.

The platform was filled with low tables, each with rows of cushions on both sides. Falendans of all ages stood beside the cushions.

Then I saw the food, and everything else became a blur. Platters loaded with golden wheels like cheeses sat next to steaming loaves. Wooden bowls held what I took for fruits and vegetables in jewel-like tones of emerald, ruby, and sapphire, but with odd, contorted shapes. Beyond them were tiny eggs boiled in their speckled-fuchsia shells, and mounds of pastries that looked light enough to fly. But there was nothing that looked or smelled like meat.

Nitana led me to the head of the nearest table. Meli, moving as if she already knew what was expected of her, took her place at its foot.

"Brothers and sisters," Nitana thought to the crowd, "our sister Mélikulénduliminála of Kalotelaméliku has brought to us the Deliverer we have all awaited so long. We are privileged to have him in our midst. Let us hail our Deliverer!"

The people bowed in synchrony, like a well-rehearsed chorus line, then gazed at me. For one panicked moment I was afraid they might expect me to give a speech. But Nitana held up her hand, and the Falendans began a song—some kind of table grace, I figured. The song lasted just long enough for me to forget my hunger in its ringing polyphony. Then they all fell silent, sat, and began their meal.

I set to with a will. Each food I tried was more scrumptious than the last. The fruits with the most gnarled gourd-like shapes turned out to be the sweetest. But Lodamor's brooding gaze fixed on me from across the table was almost enough to turn them sour.

His thought-voice broke in on me in the middle of a bite. "Where did you come from?"

I looked up at him. "A planet called Earth. Don't suppose you've heard of it?" I had a vision of rows of small lavender-skinned children in grey flannel uniforms, chanting, "Mercury, Venus, Earth, Mars . . ."

"No, I have not." Lodamor's eyes bored into me. "Why did you come here?"

"You mean to Falenda? I didn't come on purpose. I was brought."

"Brought! By whom?"

I shrugged. "The elúndina. Or so they tell me."

Lodamor picked at the peel of a mottled chartreuse-and-indigo fruit. "Why should the Deliverer be a foreigner? I would go to the City myself, and so would any man here. What can you do that we cannot?"

I sat back and threw up my hands. "You got me there, mate. I'm not clear on that bit myself."

Frustration seeped from Lodamor's pores. I leaned forward on my elbows. "Look, Lodamor, this whole thing was not my idea. If I could trade places with you, I would. But that doesn't seem to be the plan."

He looked up at me, and for the first time the resentment drained from his eyes. "The plan. Yes. Neither you nor I can make our own plans."

His eyes strayed toward Meli with an expression I didn't like. "The plan is that Meli and I will someday marry. But if she does not come back from the City alive—"

I felt as if I'd been punched in the stomach. "Marry? You and Meli? But she's so—" I swallowed. So beautiful, so unapproachable, so pure. "She's so young," I finished lamely.

"It is the tradition for the families of logosagami to intermarry so that the gift will be passed on. Meli and I are the only children of our generation. And the difference in our ages is not so great." His mouth quirked. "I must confess, though, the waiting does grow irksome at times."

I looked away. It was a good thing Lodamor had the manners not to eavesdrop on my thoughts, because he would not have liked what he heard.

When it was time to get up from the table, I could hardly stand. I wouldn't have thought it possible for me to get stiffer than when I first dismounted, but I had. Nitana noticed and thought something to Lodamor.

Lodamor showed me to a stone-lined pool surrounded by curtains at the base of the tree. It was full of a clear, steaming liquid that smelled like—well, like comfort. "This is calivóda," he told me. "You may bathe here. It will heal your soreness."

He left me, and I had the greatest bath of my life. By the time I finished, I not only wasn't sore anymore, I felt like I could leap up to the dining platform in a single bound. I didn't try it, though.

In one day I'd had a taste of out-of-this-world singing, the most delicious and satisfying food ever, a stuff-of-dreams tree-house, and a miracle bath. This would have been the life—if it hadn't been for Hakagrug.

CHAPTER NINE

In Which I Become a Vegetarian

I SPENT THE NIGHT IN A PERFECT little bower—a bed nestled into the crook of two branches and curtained on all sides by thick orange foliage. We woke early, and the tree-villagers saw us off with breakfast, songs, and good wishes.

I kept my eye on Meli and Lodamor as they said goodbye, but they parted like neutral acquaintances. If anything, Meli was on the cool side with him. After that I breathed a little easier. "There's many a slip 'twixt the cup and the lip," my granny used to say—I bet arranged marriages get spilled all the time.

Soon we were back in the endless meadow. We trotted a bit, then walked a bit, so I could build up endurance. During one of our walking breaks, I said as casually as I could, "So I understand you and Lodamor already knew each other."

Meli tossed her head. "Oh, yes. I have known him almost since I was born."

What did that head-toss mean? "He seemed like an okay guy, once he got over resenting me."

"He is a hothead, and if he does not learn to control his

temper, he will come to grief." Meli's mouth was set, and her eyes glittered like cold steel instead of gold.

"So . . . it sounds like you're not really looking forward to marrying him."

She raised her chin. "There will be no marriage."

My heart did a double back flip at that, but I told it sternly to pipe down. I couldn't have her sensing my reaction. "But what about the tradition?"

"Traditions can be changed." With that Meli pressed her knees to Nila's sides and set off at a trot. The subject was closed.

Fine by me. I knew all I needed to know. I asked Vali to trot and enjoyed the wind in my hair.

The day was like a perfect summer day in England—the kind we get about twice a year. I turned off my worry-brain and drank in the strange beauty of the world around me—the violet grasses parting under Vali's feet, the graceful loveliness of Meli and Nila trotting ahead of me. An idyllic day—if only we weren't traveling into certain danger. The worry-brain rebooted.

After several hours of wrestling with the worry-brain for control of the on-switch, I saw movement in the distance. A glimmer of light shot off a few tall figures. All around them were shorter things that looked like animated cloaks—too broad to be children. "What are those?" I asked Meli silently.

"The lucáfu herders and their flocks. It is from the lucáfu wool that our cloaks and all our fabrics are made."

When I figured it was about noon—the gold of the sky at its most intense—we got close enough for me to see the herders clearly. Meli hailed them aloud. In thought-speech they invited us to join them for lunch.

When we had dismounted with their help (I didn't fall in anyone's lap this time), Meli introduced me as the Deliverer, and all the herders bowed. I wished they wouldn't do that. I hadn't delivered anybody yet.

The herders sat cross-legged on the ground. I lowered myself next to them, stifling a groan. My calivóda bath had worn off, and I was almost as sore as I had been the night before.

The two balikuni set to grazing along with the lucáfu. All the animals were using their long tongues to pick out fallen, brownish stems of grass, avoiding the living grass itself.

The lucáfu looked more or less like goats, but with silky, shimmering coats that fell almost to their feet. When they grazed, they looked like moving tents. They were docile as sheep, and as the herders were getting the meal ready, one of them went to milk one of the animals. He offered me some of the warm fresh milk in a malacána-wood cup, along with a big slab of bread and cheese.

I took a tiny taste of the milk and then drank deeply. Like everything on Falenda, it was delicious. "Is the cheese made from this milk?" I asked the herder in my mind.

"Of course," he answered. "What else would one make cheese from?"

"Well, on my world, we have several kinds of animals that give milk. The milk we mostly drink and make cheese from comes from big animals called cows. They don't have any wool."

The herder's eyebrows rose. "You have animals that serve you in only one way?"

"Not exactly. We also turn their skin into leather to make things with. And of course we eat them."

Instant silence filled my mind. All the Falendans stared at me as if I'd confessed to cannibalism.

Meli was the first to recover. "We must remember, my brothers, that our Deliverer comes from a Flattened world. They have many ways that would seem strange to us. They are not brothers with all their animals as we are here."

The herders dropped their shocked eyes and went on with their meal, but they didn't speak to me again. I could feel their wariness in my mind, as if they feared I might take a bite out of a lucáfu at any moment.

What was I doing here? How could I be a deliverer for these people when I couldn't even measure up to their basic rules of life?

After a few centuries of silence, Meli asked the herders if they had any news from the City or anywhere along the way.

"Not news, exactly," I heard the reply. "But the shadow of the mountains is spreading. The lucáfu are restless, especially at night. We do not like to sleep without shelter. The nikhi are abroad."

"Do you know of any place we can shelter, four or five hours' ride from here?"

"There is a small community in a cavern. But you will have to announce yourselves ahead of time. The cavern is well hidden, and they are wary of travelers. You must arrive before dusk or they may not take you in."

When we'd eaten and said goodbye, Meli and I mounted our balikuni—this time almost smoothly on my part—and rode on. Meli said silently, "It will be better, I think, if you do not speak much of your own world. It is difficult for my people to understand the ways of the Flattened Ones."

"Right. I noticed at dinner last night there wasn't any meat, but I didn't think about you never eating it at all."

"We do not eat or destroy any living thing. We do not pick

the fruits and vegetables; when they ripen, they fall from the trees or vines, and we gather them. Even the animals do not eat the living grasses—did you notice? They pick out the dead stems. And the wood we use for carving is all deadfall. We never cut a living tree."

That did it. No way could I be the deliverer of this bright, clear, harmonious world. I might not be Flattened, but I felt about two inches high.

CHAPTER TEN

In Which We Talk About the Weather

W E RODE FOR A COUPLE more hours across the meadow with the forest marching along at our right hand, about half a mile away. Then in the distance I saw something I hadn't yet seen in Falenda—clouds. At least, I assumed they were clouds. The sky ahead was dark and roiling, and the darkness was moving toward us—fast.

Meli's nousíniki waved like a startled jellyfish. "A carfánu storm. We must make for the forest. Quickly!" She touched Nila's neck. Nila veered to the right and shot forward in a gallop.

I signaled Vali to follow. "What are you so worried about? So what if we get a little wet?"

"Wet? A carfánu storm is not rain. Hurry!"

Vali broke into a gallop. We'd never practiced this. I dug my knees into Vali's sides and my fingers into his mane, leaned forward over his neck, and hung on like a bull terrier to a stick.

We were paces away from the trees when the storm broke. Not rain, indeed. Fierce wind propelling golf-ball-sized pellets that looked like scarlet hail. Then one hit Nila's neck with a sickening sizzle. I caught a glimpse of singed hair and reddened flesh. Nila honked wildly and reared, pawing the air. Meli hung on with her fingers twined in Nila's mane as Nila plunged and pivoted, mad with pain and terror.

I turned Vali back, dodging flameballs right and left. *Calm down, Nila,* I thought to her. *It's all right, girl. We'll take care of you, but we've got to get under the trees. Just a little farther now.* I grabbed at her horn as she whipped her head around, trying to get hold of it without losing an eye. Finally I succeeded and held her with my eyes. *There now. It's all right.*

Nila stopped bucking, though her breathing was ragged. Her eyes rolled as a rock sizzled to the ground, just missing her foot. *Come on, now, Nila. Follow Vali under the trees, there's a good girl.* Vali whickered and nuzzled Nila's cheek with his nose.

Keeping close to her side, Vali and I urged Nila forward. We raced into the shelter of the forest as a clump of burning rocks singed Vali's tail.

Meli lay slumped over Nila's neck, fingers still gripping her curly mane, breathing hard. "Meli? Are you all right?" I reached out to touch her shoulder.

She straightened slowly. "I am not hurt," she managed. "I shall be well shortly. Thank you, Danny. You acted with great presence of mind."

She seemed surprised at this, but I could forgive her. I was a little surprised myself.

I looked up. "Are we really safe in here? These trees can't be impenetrable."

"The malacána make a thick, strong canopy. If the carfánu do get through, they lose their heat and their speed before they reach the ground. But we must stay close to the trunks to be fully protected. And that is where the nikhi are most likely to hide."

We dismounted under the largest malacána we could find, using its gnarled roots for a dismounting block. From her belt-pouch Meli produced a small emerald-green flask. She poured a drop of pale-green fluid on Nila's wound. Before my eyes, the blistered skin smoothed and faded from crimson to tan, and the now-orange coat grew back to cover it.

I blinked in disbelief. "Is that a whaddyacallit—those crystal things you told me about?"

71

"The flask is made of lenafálina, yes. The liquid absorbs its healing property."

"Wow. If I had some of that, I'd face down Bull any day of the week." Immediately I wished I hadn't let that thought into the front of my mind.

She cocked her head at me. "What is 'Bull'?"

"It's a who. Sort of. But never mind." I wasn't going to reveal my habitual cowardice now, when she'd just begun to see me as a hero.

The storm went on for hours. A few rocks fell through the foliage, but as Meli predicted, they'd lost their heat and momentum. "Why don't the carfánu set the trees on fire?"

"The malacána have much moisture in their foliage. They do not easily burn."

I looked up into the tree above me. I hadn't paid much attention to the foliage when we rode through the forest before, and it had been too dark for me to see clearly last night, when I'd slept in the bower. The foliage didn't really look like leaves, but more like huge, orange dandelion clocks that were indeed glistening with moisture.

"What causes carfánu storms, anyway? Is it something to do with Hakagrug?"

"In a sense, yes. Hakagrug's awakening stirred the deeps of Falenda. Now from time to time the hot rock from the roots of the mountains erupts out of the mine shafts, and the wind carries it for many miles. The carfánu itself is part of what forms the lenafálina. It is not evil. It is only out of its proper place."

When the wind had died down, Meli moved out of the trees' shelter to check the sky. "It is dusk now. We will not be able to reach the cavern the herders spoke of. We will have to camp here."

I'd enjoyed camping the few times I'd had the chance, but in the English countryside, the biggest danger is the occasional marauding fox. I hadn't met any nikhi face to face, but I was pretty sure a whole army of foxes would be preferable. Maybe even an army of bears. If a thing has teeth and claws, at least you can shoot it. But it sounded like nikhi mostly attacked the mind, and I had no clue how to fight something like that.

Meli sensed my nervousness. "We have a tent, and I will keep watch so that my nousíniki will give us light. If I sleep, their light will go out." Her nousíniki were glowing softly already.

I took a few deep breaths and followed her out to the edge of the meadow, where we cleared a space of the cooled carfánu. We unpacked the tent and set it up on its malacána-wood poles. Vali and Nila grazed nearby, as placidly as if the storm had never happened. Apparently nikhi didn't worry them.

We sat on the ground with a flat rock for a table and made a meal of melikunápitu with dried fruit and cheese. Then Meli said, "Sleep, Danny. I will watch."

"But you need sleep too, don't you?"

"I can watch for one night with no ill effect. Tomorrow I hope we will find safer shelter."

I wrapped myself in my cloak and lay down, determined to wake after a few hours and let her sleep. It just wasn't chivalrous to leave a lady to do all the watching. And anyway, how could I sleep when every shadow might conceal a nikhi and every muscle clamored for a calivóda bath and a nice soft bed?

CHAPTER ELEVEN

In Which I Light a Candle and Curse the Darkness

I RAN THROUGH A MAZE OF dark streets between high, windowless cliffs of stone, calling for my mother. I had to find her before I shattered the Dome. "Mum, Mum!" I cried, but my voice made no echo, and I realized I was only calling in my mind. My mother wouldn't hear my thoughts—she'd been Flattened. I opened my mouth to cry aloud, but no sound came out. Desperately I fumbled in my pouch for the music box and opened it. The cylinder turned but made no music. The City had silenced us both.

I woke with a start to see the tent walls faintly lit by Meli's nousíniki. The light faded as her head began to nod, then brightened as she jerked upright.

"Meli, let me watch awhile. You're falling asleep."

She shook herself and widened her eyes at me. "I am awake. What is the point in you watching? If I sleep, we will have no light."

"I have matches—maybe even a candle in my pouch." I touched the music box first, relieved it was at least still there. Then I pulled out a book of paper matches and a thick candle stub about two inches long. "This should last a couple of hours, anyway."

Meli picked up the candle and examined it from all sides. "What is the purpose of this thing?"

I started to laugh, then remembered we had to be quiet. "It gives light," I thought to her. For once, I knew more about something than she did. "Here, I'll show you." I ripped a match from the book and struck it, then held it to the wick. The candle began to glow with a golden flame.

Meli drew back in alarm. "You carry fire in your pouch?"

"Not fire, just an easy way to make it." I dripped a little wax onto the flat rock we'd used for a table and stuck the candle down on it. "How do you make fire?"

"We do not make it. It is given to us. Every year on the eve of the High Feast of the Great One, all our fires are doused. Then during the ceremony of the feast, the fire in the great hall comes to life again. I think it is the elúndina that kindle it. All the people take this fire to their dwellings, and it burns until the next feast. But we have no use for a little fire such as you have made. It does not provide enough heat to cook a meal or warm a cold night."

"No. But it does make enough light to chase away the darkness so you can go to sleep."

"Yes." Meli smiled. "Out here in the open land with the nikhi about, your—candle, did you call it?—is a useful thing. I will sleep a little while. Thank you."

Meli lay down, and her nousíniki dimmed into darkness. I was left alone with the candle and the memory of my dream.

It was only a dream, but the chill of those dark stone streets had entered my bones, and the candle's brave but tiny flame wasn't enough to warm them. I held my hands over it and shivered. I looked over at Meli, sleeping soundly under her cloak. It was all very well for her to sleep, but what about me, left with only a candle for company and protection against the nikhi? The candle lit only the middle of the tent.

From the corner of my eye, in the shadows above Meli's sleeping body, I thought I saw movement. When I looked full at the place, there was only seamless darkness. *It must have been the candle flickering,* I told myself. But I didn't believe it. Fear crept into me like a parasite and began to gnaw at my guts.

My worry-brain went into high gear, thinking about what the next day might bring. Today I'd ridden almost to the point of paralysis, been ostracized by a bunch of vegetarian Falendans, narrowly escaped being scorched or pummeled to death by flaming rocks, and been stranded at night near a forest seething with unseen enemies. What worse things might overtake me tomorrow?

Why should I go through this for a bunch of people who clearly thought I was a barbarian? What if it was all a lie about me being the only one who could break the power of the Dome? Maybe they just didn't want to send more of their own people into danger. After all, what sense did it make that an ordinary kid could deliver a whole planet? I was ordinary, despite what the logosagami said. In fact, I was less than ordinary—I was a nobody from a poor non-family, with no brains, no brawn, and a voice that might break any minute. What if it broke when I was trying to sing down the Dome? I'd be trapped in the City forever, Flattened into nothingness, just like my mum. I'd never be able to save her. It was all a pointless fraud.

I stared at the candle flame until my eyes burned and my heart twisted inside me. Just outside the flame, the shadows cavorted, making hideous gargoyle shapes against the tent walls. The air grew close and breathless.

Then I decided: I wouldn't do it. I would not sacrifice myself for nothing. I'd go back to the place I landed when I fell from the tower and find some way to get home.

The shadows leapt and danced about me as I got up and started cramming things into my saddlebags. They weren't behaving like normal shadows at all, but by this point I didn't care. Whatever the nikhi might do, I didn't see how it could be worse than what their enemies, the elúndina, had already let me in for.

I tried to be quiet, but in my hurry I knocked the bag against a tent-pole. It creaked, and Meli woke up.

"Danny, what are you doing?"

"I'm getting out of here. I can't do this, and there's no point killing myself trying. You go ahead if you want. I'm going back."

"Are you mad? You will not survive ten minutes outside in the darkness. And what about your mother?"

That was a low blow, but it glanced off me. "I can't help her. She's probably dead by now. All you people want is to send me to the grave after her. Well, I'm not having it. I'm going home."

Meli rose to her knees, and her nousíniki waved toward me. "Danny, these are not your thoughts. The nikhi have penetrated your mind. You must resist them!"

Her words sat on the surface of my mind like lily pads on a pond. I couldn't take them in. My brain felt like some viscous goo I might create in science class. All I knew was I had to get away. I bent to fasten the straps of the saddlebag, then straightened with it over my shoulder. I pulled back the flap of the tent.

Meli called out in her chiming voice, and I heard in my mind, "Elúndina! Help us!"

I looked back and saw the candle flame leap up to ten times its former size. It burned white-hot, but every color of the spectrum flickered within that white flame. The shadows cowered away from it. I wanted to cover my eyes, or run, but my hands and feet wouldn't move. I was rooted between horror and a sharp joy that pierced my heart.

The joy spoke to me in tones that penetrated the fog in my mind. It reminded me of the old days when my mother was still with me, when life was a series of childish adventures punctuated with moments of that same joy—finding a new butterfly, listening to Mum's lullabies, stargazing from the bell tower. What had I been thinking? Even if it was hopeless, I had to try to save Mum.

I could hardly believe what I saw next. Bits of the flame broke off and shot up to the roof of the tent. But it didn't catch fire. The flame-bits took wings, each a different color, and at last I recognized them: elúndina. They fluttered into every dark corner, driving winged bits of shadow out of them. I knew at once those shadow-bits were nikhi.

Now that I saw them clearly, I wondered that I could ever have mistaken them for mere shadows. They weren't just black—they were like bits of emptiness carved out of the fabric of the universe, as black as if they'd sucked up every bit of light that ever was and killed it. But they couldn't suck up the elúndina.

The elúndina swelled and blazed with a light too bright to look at as they clashed wings with the nikhi. I crouched with my hands over my head as the battle raged around me. At last the nikhi gave a great collective shriek and zoomed past me into the night.

When they were gone, the elúndina—dimmed now to their normal size and brightness—fluttered gently around me. Gradually my churning thoughts grew quiet. I felt drained, empty, but at peace. The elúndina hovered for a moment, as if to say goodbye, then flew back to the candle and melted into its flame.

CHAPTER TWELVE
In Which Pride Goes Before a Fall

MELI BLEW OUT THE CANDLE. "We should save this for another night."

I stared at the thin wisp of smoke rising from the smoldering wick. I couldn't look Meli in the eye. I'd been on the point of deserting her, and she'd saved me.

"It will be light soon," she thought to me. "If you feel able, we should break our fast and move on. We have much ground to cover today to make up for what we lost in the storm."

"Meli—" My thoughts stuttered. "About what happened—"

"There is nothing to say about what happened."

"But—I almost deserted you. I did—what do you call it? Misamárila."

She shook her head. "No. That was not you acting. That was the nikhi."

"But I would've gone if you hadn't stopped me."

"Not I. The elúndina. Listen, Danny. How do you feel now? Do you still mean to turn back?"

I searched my heart. It still cowered, trembling, like me

80

when Dad's on a rampage; but I was more ashamed of turning back than afraid of going on. "No. I'm committed to this, whatever happens."

"There, you see? Those were not altogether your own thoughts you were thinking. The nikhi got into your mind and played upon your fear and doubt. Then the elúndina healed you, and now you are yourself again. There is nothing to repent of. Only now you must learn to resist the nikhi's attacks."

"How do I do that?" How could I resist an enemy I could neither see, nor hear, nor feel? One I could punch, now, that would be a different matter.

"You must be alert for any sign of fear or discouragement. If you detect such a thought, you must immediately cry out to the elúndina for help."

"But what if we get stuck in the dark again? My candle's almost gone. I saw the elúndina—they came out of the flame. How can they come if we're in total darkness?"

"There is no darkness so complete that the elúndina cannot materialize. If nothing else, they can use the light of the stars. Do not worry so much, Danny. Trust me. The Great One will protect us."

Always the Great One. Trusting him was all very well for the Falendans. But all he'd done for me so far was to rip me out of my familiar world and dump me in the greatest danger I'd ever known.

WE RODE THROUGH THE MEADOW all morning, trotting as much as the balikuni and I could stand. By the time we stopped for lunch, I could see a dark shape on the horizon. I pointed. "That's not another storm, is it?"

Meli followed my finger with her eyes. "No. Those are the mountains."

"*The* mountains? The ones we're going to?"

"There are no others."

"How long will it take to get there?"

"If all goes well, we should reach the base of the mountains by midday tomorrow. If we had not been delayed by the storm, I would have said tonight. We have lost half a day."

Midday tomorrow! Late we might be, but midday tomorrow was still much too soon for comfort.

In the course of the afternoon we met up with another group of lucáfu herders with their flocks. Meli greeted them and introduced me as the Deliverer. Their response was considerably cooler than I'd come to expect.

"He looks like a Flattened One to me," thought the oldest of the herders.

"He has that appearance because he is from another world," Meli explained. "He is not Flattened. He can use thought-speech just as we can."

I took this cue to think to the man, "It's true. I know I don't look the part, but the logosagami says I really am the Deliverer."

The herder grunted. His nousíniki, which seemed duller and limper than Meli's, moved their tips lazily in my direction. He made no further objection, but he still looked wary.

Meli asked if he knew of a place we could spend the night.

"There's a village about two hours' ride from here," the herder replied. "But I doubt they'll take you in. They don't take kindly to strangers."

Meli's nousíniki waved. "Strangers! What kind of talk is that to use among True Falendan brothers?"

The herder jerked his head at me. "He's no True Falendan, whatever you may be."

Meli drew herself tall on Nila's back. "I am Mélikulénduliminála, the granddaughter of the logosagami of Kalotelaméliku. I am of the Blood."

"Well, miss, begging your pardon, but that's as may be. You have the golden eyes and all, but we don't know you, and around here we stick to our own."

Meli's whole body tautened and her eyes seemed about to flash fire at the man. I didn't know if she had any such power, but I didn't want to find out. "Well, thanks for your help," I thought to the herder. "We'll be on our way now."

I told Vali to walk on. After a few paces I looked back and was relieved—and a little surprised—to find Meli and Nila following. I stopped to let them catch up.

"Thank you, Danny. I am afraid I was about to lose my temper with that man."

I bit back a smile. *About* to lose her temper? That was a good one.

I gave her some time to cool down, then thought to her, "What'll we do for the night? Go to that village and take a chance?"

"Certainly we will. That herder was clearly an ignorant man. No village of True Falendans would ever turn away one of the Blood."

I hesitated. "Of course I don't know, but—is it possible they're not completely True Falendans any more? I mean, didn't those herders' nousíniki seem a little limp to you?"

Meli stopped Nila in her tracks and stared at me.

"Did I say something wrong?"

She shook her head. "You said something remarkably right.

83

You are very perceptive, Danny. You saw what I did not see, blinded by my pride in the Blood. It is true. All those herders' nousíniki were beginning to weaken." She started Nila at a walk again. "I must think further of this. It may not be safe to visit that village after all."

When the golden sky began to fade, Meli said, "Let us look for a good spot to camp—near the forest, but not too near."

I looked around. The violet meadow stretched flat in all directions; the forest marched along an even distance to our right. What could make one place better than another?

We rode on a bit, with no change in the landscape that I could see. Then Meli's nousíniki began to wave, and she said, "Stop here. Someone is coming."

A tall Falendan woman emerged from the trees and stopped just at the edge of the forest. The hood of her cloak was pulled up over her head, which I thought was funny since the afternoon was still warm.

The woman raised her arm. "Hail, Deliverer!" she cried in the tinkling Falendan speech.

It seemed a bit odd that she was speaking aloud, but then Meli often greeted people aloud as well. What was odder was that she called me Deliverer before we'd been introduced.

"And hail, Child of the Blood!"

Meli smiled and thought to me, "You see, there are some True Falendans left in this far end of the meadow." She urged Nila closer, and Vali followed, though I was inclined to hang back.

She said aloud, "Hail, my sister. Are you from the village we have heard tell of in these parts?"

The woman nodded. "I am their logosagami. We welcome you to Telamalacánu, the Village of the Trees."

We were close enough now for me to see the woman's face under her hood as she turned to me. Her eyes were golden like Meli's, but something seemed wrong. They had a hard glitter, not the soft luster of Meli's eyes, and there was no life behind them.

"Be careful, Meli," I thought to her. "I don't trust this woman. I think she's a fake."

Meli turned to me. "Do not be ridiculous, Danny. Clearly she is of the Blood. Look at her eyes."

"That's just what I mean—they're all wrong! Can't you tell? And why is she wearing a hood when it's warm and dry? She's hiding something." Vali and Nila both honked and pawed at the ground. "See? Even the balikuni feel it. There's evil here. And look at her. She doesn't understand our thoughts." The woman was looking from Meli to me, brow furrowed in concentration, as if she could catch the tune but not the words.

Meli frowned. "I am certain there is some explanation," she thought to me. Then aloud to the woman she said, "I am Mélikulénduliminála of Kalotelaméliku, and this is Danny, our Deliverer. We seek shelter for the night. Can you accommodate us?"

The woman turned her hard golden eyes on me. They narrowed only slightly, but the wave of hatred they shot out toward me rocked me in my seat. Still, she responded in the same sweetly chiming voice as before. "Most certainly. Please, follow me."

Meli signaled Nila to walk forward, but I laid a hand on her arm. "Meli, don't go with her. I'm sure she means us harm, I can feel it."

Meli looked at me, her eyes clouded in confusion. "But why would she?"

"Because she's Flattened! Can't you sense it? I bet she's spying for Hakagrug. Meli, we've got to get out of here!" I turned Vali back into the meadow, expecting Meli to follow.

She hesitated a moment too long. Behind me I heard the woman's voice clashing like cymbals: "Nikhi! After them!"

CHAPTER THIRTEEN

In Which I Get in Touch with My Inner Boy Scout

LIKE A SWARM OF MAN-EATING black moths from hell, bits of tree-shadow broke away from the forest and rushed at Meli. She seemed too stunned to move. *Nila! Run!* I thought, and Vali backed me up with a frantic honk. Nila hesitated, torn between her mate and her mistress. The air filled with the flapping of dark wings, and the temperature plummeted. At last Nila broke toward the meadow in a gallop.

Vali needed no urging to run his fastest. I was glued to his back, the two of us moving like one animal. Fear mounted in my throat—wild, irrational, paralyzing fear. All I could think of was galloping, fast and hard.

I turned to look at Meli, just behind me, then watched helplessly as the nikhi surrounded her. Her eyes went wild, her mouth opened in a scream, her arms flailed about her head. Nila's pace hadn't slackened. In another minute Meli might fall off her back.

Then, suddenly, Meli's face went blank. She slumped over Nila's neck, leaning to the right. Her arm trailed almost to the ground as she jounced with Nila's gallop, slipping, slipping—

In a panic, I tried to turn Vali back toward her, but he was running too fast. I didn't know what to do. If Nila kept galloping, Meli would fall. If she stopped, the nikhi would take Meli over completely.

And then at last I remembered what to do in a nikhi attack. "Elúndina! Help us!" I cried with all the breath I could muster.

Ahead of me, with a sound like trumpets, the fading golden light shattered into prisms. The colors of the prism resolved into bits of light like fluttering wings. A huge corps of elúndina rushed toward us, past us, enveloping us in a roar of warmth. Light wings and dark wings swirled together like a cloud of angry wasps.

It was like watching a battle film, except that I could feel the beaten air swirling about me, taste the acrid bite of fear in my throat, smell the putrid stink of the nikhi against the fresh, bracing scent of the elúndina. The center elúndina made a circle around Meli, cutting off the nikhi that surrounded her, while the right and left flanks closed in on the battalion of nikhi following behind.

More nikhi swooped in from the forest to swell the enemy ranks. The elúndina flanks were pushed back, leaving the detachment surrounding Meli cut off from the rest. I watched with my breath stopped in my throat. Surely the elúndina could never be defeated?

I longed to help, but what could I do? I poured my soul into a prayer for Meli's safety. Then the whole sky exploded into wings of light. Rank upon rank of elúndina dove down on the nikhi like eagles intent on their prey. Each elúndina swelled in size and brightness until all I could see was a wall of light forcing the darkness back and back, past Nila and Meli, all the way to the border of the forest. The shriek of the vanquished nikhi rent the air with a last spasm of terror, then wailed away like a siren into the trees.

Exhausted, the balikuni slowed to a trot. But before I could grab Nila, Meli slipped from her back to the ground, and I heard a sickening crunch. Nila, carried helplessly on by her own momentum, had stepped on her mistress's leg.

"Meli!" I pulled Vali to a halt, jumped off his back, and ran to Meli's side. Nila honked hysterically and nuzzled Meli with her horn. A platoon of elúndina, now back to butterfly size, fluttered round her while the main army melted back into the sky.

I knelt beside Meli. Her leg was blotched with violet and deep purple, and twisted at an angle no leg should be. I gritted my teeth and cursed myself. Why hadn't I paid attention in first aid class?

"The flask," I heard in my mind—the far-off echoing voice of the elúndina. "The lenafálina flask."

I jumped up and rummaged in Nila's saddlebags. "Where in blazes is it?"

"Her pouch."

I knelt by Meli again and yanked her belt-pouch open. There it was—the green flask. "Do I put it on her leg or make her drink it?" I muttered. No reply from the elúndina, so I did both—one drop on her leg and one in her mouth. The flask was nearly empty.

I expected the immediate results I'd seen on Nila the day before, but no such luck. The bruising faded a little, but the leg didn't straighten and Meli didn't wake. "Come on, come on," I urged her. She was so pale it hurt to look at her. I took her hand and chafed it between my own. It was as cold as the wind of the nikhi.

"Can't you help her?" I cried to the elúndina.

They fluttered around her. "She has been wounded by the nikhi as well as by the fall," they told me. "We can restore her mind, but it will take time. Her leg we cannot help. Give her more of the lenafálina, and cover her with her cloak."

I poured another drop onto her leg, then upended the flask and shook it. It was dry.

I laid the cloak over her. There must be more I could do. Come on, brain—what do you do for a broken leg? A splint! I whipped my head around. Where in this wilderness of grass could I possibly find a stick of wood?

The tent.

I unrolled the tent and grabbed the shortest of the poles, broke off a piece the length of Meli's calf, then used my pocket-knife to rip a narrow strip off the bottom of the covering. I still wished I'd paid better attention in first aid class, but at least I'd seen enough action films to manage a rough splint—if only I didn't make a hash of it. With shaking hands I eased the bone straight, fighting down nausea as the ragged ends clicked into place. Then I bound her leg tightly to the pole.

Meli gave a low moan, but didn't wake. I pulled the cloak over her.

A few minutes later, her eyelids fluttered. The elúndina retreated a few feet. "She will waken now. Her mind is healed. Do not fear. We will keep watch with you."

"Meli?" I whispered. "Can you hear me?"

Her eyes opened and she tried to sit up, then fell back with a groan. "Danny? What happened?"

I gave her the condensed version. "And I'm afraid your leg's broken."

"The flask—did you use the flask?"

I nodded. "Didn't seem to help much."

She sighed painfully. "Bones do not heal easily, even with lenafálina. But you have done well, Danny. Thank you."

I brought my saddlebag and put it under her head, then took her hand again. It was still cold, but not as icy as before. "Is it bad?"

"It is bearable. The lenafálina serves to reduce the pain." She lay silent a while, then, "How did you know?"

"Well—first I wondered why she had her hood up. I thought it might be to hide Flattened nousíniki. And she just felt evil to me. But what clinched it was her eyes. They looked all wrong, kind of hard and dead. This might sound daft, but in my world people can put things over their eyes to make them look a different color. Contact lenses, they call them. And I wondered if she might have made fake lenses out of some kind of golden crystal."

Meli's thoughts came slowly. "The golden lenafálina have the power to affect the mind. They are hardly ever used among the True Falendans—only to heal a mind that is diseased. But if she put them over her eyes, as you say, that would explain how she had me almost hypnotized." A long pause, and then Meli gave my hand a feeble squeeze. "You saved my life, Danny."

I managed a shaky smile. "Looks like we're even, then."

She was still way too pale. "You'd better get some rest," I told her. "I'll watch, and the elúndina said they would stay with us tonight."

Meli sighed and closed her eyes. She was so fragile and

helpless, like a newborn baby. I touched one finger lightly to her cheek. Not only would I be helpless in this strange land without her, I'd be lonely too.

Feeling foolish, I pressed my lips to her sleeping hand. "Get well, Meli."

As night closed in, the cold closed in as well. I took a long drink of melikunápitu, then wrapped myself in my cloak and lay down beside Meli. Vali and Nila came next to us, one on each side, and folded their legs underneath them like cats. I snuggled into their warmth.

Even with the animals for company and the elúndina fluttering above us, I couldn't sleep. It didn't take a nikhi attack to make me dread what the next day would bring. It was clear now there would be no safe shelter so close to the mountains. If Meli wasn't healed enough to ride by morning, what would we do? We should have reached the mountains by now. We had only five days to go before Moon Merge.

For that matter, what would we do if and when we reached the City? No one had bothered to explain that minor detail. Apparently we'd have to improvise. I shivered. I'm a classical chorister, not a jazz musician. I could sight-read a Bach cantata, but I'd never improvised a note in my life.

CHAPTER FOURTEEN

In Which I Learn to Improvise

As soon as it was light, the elúndina fluttered around us as if saying goodbye, then vanished into the pale golden sky. Meli and I were on our own.

Meli stirred beside me. I jumped up to fetch food from the saddlebags and turned back to see her sitting up, flexing the foot of her injured leg.

"Is it healed?" I asked her.

"Not completely. It is better, but I do not think I will be able to walk on it."

"Can you ride?"

"We shall see."

When we'd eaten, Nila knelt for Meli to mount. I helped Meli to her feet—or rather, foot—and let her lean on me while she swung her bad leg over Nila's back. Nila rose, and Meli walked her in a circle around the campsite.

I winced as Meli jolted on Nila's back. She couldn't keep her seat with one leg sticking out in a splint. "This isn't going to work," I said when she returned, her face tight with pain.

"We'll have to think of something else."

I could carry her—for about two meters. She was light, but I was no muscle-man. Or I could hold her in front of me on Vali, but her leg would still be jolted with every step.

Then it came to me. I helped her get off Nila's back and sit on the ground again. "Wait there while I fix it up."

I took the tent pieces out of the saddlebags and laid them out on the ground. First I measured a length of the fabric against Meli's body and cut it with my pocket knife a few feet longer than her height. Then I sawed and broke one of the poles into two pieces, each about a meter long. I laid one of these at each end of the strip of cloth, then poked holes in the cloth above and below the poles. Luckily, the cloth didn't ravel; it was thick and springy, like felt. I used the tent ropes to tie the cloth around the poles. Then I slung each end of the contraption around one of the balikuni's bellies. I maneuvered Vali and Nila into position so the fabric hung with just a little slack between them.

"There! What do you think?"

Meli cocked her head and stared. "What is it?"

"A hammock." I was a little hurt until I realized from her blank look they didn't have hammocks on Falenda.

Careful not to jostle her, I lifted her into the hammock and tucked a cushion of leftover tent fabric under her broken leg. Then I signaled to Vali and Nila to walk a few paces. "So how is it?"

"It will do. You are a good maker of hammocks, Danny. Where did you learn this skill?"

I shrugged. "I just improvised."

I repacked the saddlebags and slung them over the balikuni's backs. Then I realized the flaw in my plan: between the saddlebag and the rope holding the hammock, there was no room for me on Vali's back. I would have to walk.

I looked disgustedly at my rope sandals. If only I had my school brogues back! Oh, well. I'd have to walk when we reached the mountains anyway. Might as well get in some practice now.

We crawled at a tortoise pace across the meadow, the bali-kuni straining to match each other's gait and keep a constant space between them—too close and Meli's leg would be jostled painfully; too far and she might pop off. Meli didn't complain, but I could see she was uncomfortable. My feet were blistered and burning by the second mile. I was a sprinter. I had no practice at this kind of distance.

During one of our frequent rests, I asked Meli what we'd do when we reached the base of the mountains. "I do not know," she replied. "I suppose we will have to wait there until I am able to walk again. There is no point in your going on alone; you could not even enter the City without my help. But I pray I will heal quickly, for there is no time to lose."

"But won't it be dangerous?"

"It will. The nikhi will be thick there, I have no doubt, and we may meet more unfriendly Falendans as well. But the Great One will provide a way." For the first time, I heard a note of hesitation in her thoughts as she spoke of the Great One. Apparently even Meli hadn't counted on trouble like this.

I could understand why she was acting so passive, but it made me nervous. I'd become the leader of this expedition by default, and I wasn't ready for it. But if I was going to be a Deliverer, I'd have to learn to take the lead.

THE MENACING HULK THAT WAS THE MOUNTAINS got bigger and bigger, until by noon it filled the horizon. There were no foothills. All I saw was a steep, rocky face that leapt up at right angles from the plain and disappeared in a low layer of cloud. Climb that? No way.

I thought we'd never reach the base. But as the daylight faded, the forest drew in on either side, leaving a strip of meadow about a quarter of a mile wide. The grasses stopped abruptly, and graveled dirt sloped up for perhaps a hundred meters. Then the rock face began.

I stopped the balikuni at the edge of the violet grasses. Meli was grey with exhaustion, and my own feet felt like a couple of hunks of raw meat. I couldn't go another step. There wasn't enough tent left to make a full shelter; the best I'd be able to manage was a lean-to, and I didn't see much point in that. Maybe I could find a cave—but would it be safe if I did?

Before I could make up my mind, I heard a sound in the distance: a Falendan song. Meli was sunk in a state between sleep and stupor; she didn't seem to hear. The song drew closer, but now I could tell it wasn't like the Falendan songs I'd heard before: it came from a single voice.

Should I try to hide us? The only cover was in the forest, where the voice was coming from. We were camouflaged from a distance by our chameleon-like cloaks and balikuni, but we couldn't hope to hide from anyone who came near. And the voice was growing louder.

Then I remembered: The Flattened Ones didn't sing. Only True Falendans sang. Could we actually meet a friend, here at the edge of the wasteland?

A figure came out of the trees—a tall woman wearing a full-length robe. She moved like a dancer. I couldn't tell whether she had healthy nousíniki or dull, Flattened hair, because her head was covered by a globe of the same iridescent fabric as her robe. As she came closer, I could see the sphere was wrapped in layers, like a turban, and stood out several inches from her skull.

If I could have run, and Meli with me, I might have done so. This woman reminded me way too much of the false logosagami who'd set the nikhi on us the night before. But there was no way we could escape now. And then there was the singing.

The woman stopped within ten meters of us. "Hail, travelers!" her thought-voice chimed. Relief turned my knees to water so I had to lean on Vali for support. If she could speak with her thoughts, she couldn't be a fully Flattened One. "Is your companion injured? Do you seek shelter?"

"Yes, please," I thought back. "My friend, Meli, has a broken leg. We've come a long way and she's awfully tired."

"Did you say Meli?" came the voice. "I knew a girl called Meli, many years ago . . . And what are you called, boy from another world?"

I started. "How'd you know I was from another world?"

I heard her tinkling laugh. "No Falendan has such skin as yours. The Flattened Ones fade to gray, not to the color of cream. And although you lack nousíniki, yet you have the thought-speech. That is not possible for one of our world."

"Oh." I should've thought of all that. "My name is Danny. May I ask—who are you?"

Her lovely face drew inward. "Many years ago I had another name. But now I am called Márala—she who lives alone." She stretched her arm toward me. "Come, I will take you to my dwelling."

Signaling Vali and Nila to wait, I stepped close enough to

see her eyes. They were golden, with the true logosagami luster. If she was a fake, she was an awfully good fake; and I was desperate. I would have to take the chance.

I called the balikuni to follow me, then walked with Márala as she turned toward the spot where the forest came up to the mountain. We passed through a thick curtain of deep-blue tílamel vines, which made a tinkling sound as they parted and then closed behind us. Beyond these was a small clearing that held a rough pen of malacána poles. Inside the pen, a balikuni, a couple of lucáfu, and a flock of bright green bird-like creatures munched at their evening meal.

Márala lifted Meli easily from the hammock. "If you will undo that very ingenious contraption," she said, nodding to the hammock, "you may leave your balikuni here and come into my cavern." She disappeared with Meli into a cleft in the rock to the right of the pen.

I undid the hammock ropes, took off the saddlebags, and left Vali and Nila with a parting horn-scratch. The other animals moved aside to make room at the feeding trough.

I ducked through the narrow passageway in the rock and came out into a small cavern. Marala had laid Meli on a pallet in one corner. She stood unwinding the turban from her head. Underneath it were vibrant, shimmering nousíniki that immediately began to glow in the cavern's dim light. My relief was unspeakable.

"Why do you wear that thing?" I asked her.

"It protects me from the evil air that flows down from the mountain," she replied. "The tílamel vines counteract the evil, so I need not wear the turban inside."

"But why do you live right up against the mountain like this? Isn't it dangerous?"

Marala looked at me with a curious expression. "I have been waiting for someone that I knew must pass by here eventually. I think perhaps I have been waiting for you."

CHAPTER FIFTEEN

In Which Márala Tells Her Tale

I AWOKE TO A CRY FROM Meli. I leapt to my feet and thrust my hand into my pouch for my pocketknife. But when I looked toward Meli's pallet, I saw her and Márala embracing, their nousíniki twining together and glowing like a rainbow.

I stood with my mouth hanging open until they pulled apart and noticed me. Meli reached out a hand. "Danny," her thought-voice chimed, "it is my mother! She was not Flattened after all!"

I stood rooted. I was happy for Meli, but—what did this mean about *my* mum?

"Come and have breakfast, Danny," Márala thought. "I will tell you my story as you eat, and then you will learn of your mother's fate as well."

She beckoned me over to a cushion next to a low table by Meli's bed. Walking the few steps to reach it, I realized my butchered feet felt like feet again. Márala had bathed them in calivóda the night before, while I ate the supper she served me. I felt like I was staying in a posh hotel.

I sat on the cushion, and Márala spread the table with eggs, cheese, and fruit. As Meli and I ate, she told me her story.

"Seven years ago, Danny, the elúndina brought your mother Celia to us, to save Falenda from the Flattening. She was bewildered at first, as no doubt you were, and wished greatly to return home to you and your father. But she was a good woman, kind and compassionate as well as courageous, and at last we persuaded her to help us. We believed the journey could be accomplished speedily and that she could be returned to your world before she would be missed."

I nodded. Meli's grandfather had told me as much as that.

"It was necessary that a logosagami should accompany her. My father was too old to bear the rigors of the journey, so although I mourned to leave my little Meli—" She paused to touch Meli's cheek. Meli put her hand over her mother's with a quivery smile. "—Still I had to go. My husband, Falakúr, insisted on coming with us. He knew Meli would be well cared for in the village, and he could not bear to send me unprotected into danger.

"Our journey itself was uneventful. In those days the evil had not spread beyond the mountains, and there were many True Falendans to aid us along the way. It was when we reached the City that our troubles began.

"In order to enter the City, we had to disguise ourselves. It was easy to make Celia look like a Flattened One; we simply rubbed a little garama-vine juice on her skin to change the color to a Flattened gray. Falakúr and I wore turbans such as the farmers of the High Plains wear when they go into the City to sell their produce. I also had to disguise the color of my eyes, for no known logosagami would ever be allowed within the City gates. From the farmers I obtained eye-shields made of the blue lenafálina. They were intended to enhance vision and heal diseases of the eye; but they served my purposes neatly as well."

Meli and I exchanged glances, remembering the fake golden eyes of the woman in the forest.

Marala went on. "We assumed our disguises and borrowed a wagonload of fruit from the farmers. Celia hid beneath the fruit—for the Flattened Ones are not allowed to pass through the gates without a passport—and we were easily admitted into the City.

"Our task was twofold: of course we had to shatter the Dome with our singing. But before attempting that, we had to search the City for anyone who was not yet completely Flattened, to warn them of what was coming and enlist their help. The more singers we had at the fateful moment, the better our chances of success. And our attempt must be timed with the Moon Merge. This moment comes only once in every seven years, as you must know, and it is fast approaching now."

Too fast. Only four days to go.

"The fitting of my blue eye-shields had taken some time, and we arrived in the City with only three days to spare. You have not yet seen the City, but it is vast, with thousands upon thousands of poor Flattened souls imprisoned within its cliffs of stone."

I remembered my dream, crying for my mother through those stony streets. Apparently I'd dreamed something like the reality without having seen it.

"How were we to raise a chorus in three days? In our haste, we took less care than we should have. We sent out thought-messages to anyone who wore any head-covering or whose hairstyle seemed particularly buoyant. Most turned out to be Flattened Ones who simply liked hats or who teased their hair to make it stand up. They remained oblivious. A few messages did get through to those who were still able to receive them. But some were intercepted by the Enemy."

Marala's golden eyes darkened. "On the evening of the Moon Merge, we and our small band of supporters ascended the tallest building in the City, the Tower of Grozlukh, which is just at its center. The Tower was not so well guarded then as it has since become, for the Enemy had not suspected our plan ahead of time. At the top we prepared to sing. The night was dark, and although I could sense the presence of the nikhi, I could do nothing to combat them except to warn the people to guard their thoughts. The elúndina would not be able to penetrate the Dome to come to our aid."

I had a moment of panic. We'd have to confront nikhi with no elúndina to help? I glanced at Meli, then forced my mind back to Marala's story.

"Just as the moons approached the moment of merging, the nikhi struck. Only I of all our chorus was accustomed to fighting them. All the others went distracted with fear. I was able to calm some of them—Celia and Falakúr among them—and we began to sing. But by then the moment had passed. The two moons had crossed and were already beginning to separate. Our song shook the Dome but could not shatter it.

"It was then we discovered the traitors among us. I am ashamed to say there are some in the City who, although not Flattened, have willingly surrendered the powers of their nousíniki to the service of Hakagrug. Several of these had infiltrated our chorus, and when they saw that our song had failed, they captured our band and imprisoned them.

"I alone, by my power as a logosagami, was able to escape. I diverted their thoughts so they did not notice me and slipped through their midst; but I was only able to save myself."

My mind filled with a picture of malevolent hands reaching out for my mother, of faces contorted with unholy glee leering down at her as they dragged her off to some dank medieval dungeon. I swallowed hard, but the lump in my throat wouldn't budge. I wouldn't follow that picture any farther.

Marala looked like she was seeing something similar. "I stayed hidden in the City by those means for some time, searching for a way to help the captives escape. But on my own I could do nothing. I could not send my thoughts to them without the message being intercepted by Hakagrug's minions, nor could I penetrate the prison's defenses.

"At last, though it rent my heart in pieces, I had to admit defeat. I had to leave my dear friend Celia and my beloved husband, the other half of myself, and get out of the City before its evil power could begin to work on me."

Marala had deserted my mother? I would never have left her, no matter how hopeless it was. But a treacherous voice deep inside my heart said, "Oh, wouldn't you?"

Marala looked at Meli and me. "I knew that when seven years had passed, another attempt would be made to shatter the Dome. So I determined to wait here at the base of the mountains so that I could aid the new Deliverer—or receive my husband and Celia, should they manage to escape on their own. For seven years, every day at sunset I have roamed the fringes of the forest, singing, hoping to hear an answering song. And now at last, you are here."

She broke off and hugged Meli again. "My dearest daughter, how hard it has been to know that you were growing up without me! I was torn in two every moment between you and your father; but I knew you to be safe and him to be in ever-increasing danger. If he had ever managed to escape, he would have needed long and careful nursing before he could regain the strength to return home. And of course," she said, turning to look at me, "the same applies to your mother. I mourned for her also. In our short time together, she became the closest friend of my own sex I have ever known."

By this time my palms were sweating. My mother had been imprisoned for seven years. My vision of a dank medieval dungeon might fall far short of the awful truth of Hakagrug's prison. From what I'd heard, even to be what passed for free inside the City would wear anyone down in seven years. But to be imprisoned for that long . . . Would she still be alive? Would she still be my mother? Or would she be like that poor creature Velimir had brought to Meli's village, with all the life and joy and hope and singing drained out of her forever?

"There's one thing I don't understand," I said. "Everyone keeps saying I'm essential to this mission—and my mother was before me—but I still don't get exactly why. I haven't heard you talk about her doing anything you couldn't have done on your own."

Marala stared at me. "But do you not know? I thought my father would have told you. It is you who must begin the song. A song from outside our world is needed to break the Dome's power. Besides, after we have been in the City for only a day, even with turbans to protect our nousíniki, the Enemy's noise is so powerful that it chases the music from our heads. We are still able to sing, but only if someone starts the song for us. That is why we need you."

I chewed on this for a while. It was good to know there was a real reason, not just the Falendans' own cowardice. But that didn't make the task any easier. "We've lost a day already, and Meli's leg still isn't healed. Moon Merge is only four days away. We'll have even less time than you and my mother did. What if we don't make it?"

Marala's features set. "We will get there in time. I need but one day to restore Meli to health. We will start tomorrow. In two days we will reach the City. We will have only one day to assemble our choir, but I have learned much from the former attempt. I believe it will be enough."

Suddenly the day seemed brighter. "You mean you're going with us?"

"Of course. You do not think I would send two young ones—my daughter among them—into danger alone, when I am able to go with you?"

I bit my lip. I had thought just that. After all, I'd been taking care of myself, danger or no danger, pretty much since I was six. To have a mother again—even a share in someone else's mother—warmed a place inside me that had been shivering for seven years.

CHAPTER SIXTEEN

In Which I Learn the Facts of Life

M ARALA SENT ME OUTSIDE WHILE she tended Meli's leg.
"Do not go out of the clearing," she warned me. "The
nikhi are thick in the forest, and unfriendly Falendans sometimes come there as well."

But I wasn't in the mood for exploring anyway. All I could
think about was my mother. I sat on an upturned barrel and
took the Purple Emperor music box out of my belt pouch. I'd
hardly had a moment to myself since the journey began, and
somehow I didn't want to share this treasure with Meli or anyone else. I pressed the catch and eased open the lid, wishing
there was some way to turn down the volume on the music.
I didn't want Meli and Marala to hear it. But I needn't have
worried. The tinkling notes of "O Danny Boy" were nearly
drowned out by the honking, squawking, and chittering of the
animals in the pen.

"I love you, Mum," I whispered to her picture inside the lid.
"I'm coming to rescue you. And Marala is too. Just hang on."

I kissed the picture, then put the box away and strolled

over to visit the animals. Vali and Nila were happily munching their breakfast of dried grass. I scratched their horns, then did the same for Marala's balikuni, who came nosing up to me as well. The birdlike creatures—Marala called them búrika—strutted their brilliant green plumage before me and made clicking noises with their weird triangular beaks.

The lucáfu butted their heads gently against my hand, and I stroked their shimmering wool. They chittered to me, and I wondered if they might want milking. As I thought this, their chittering crescendoed. They'd read my thoughts.

I'm a city boy. I'd never milked anything in my life. But how hard could it be? I'd mastered a lot of new skills since I came to Falenda.

I found a stool and a bucket in one corner of the pen and went back to the lucáfu. The smaller one was waiting for me on a low platform, while the other hovered nearby. I sat on the stool, parted the animal's long wool, and put the bucket under its udder. Then I grabbed one of the six teats and pulled.

Nothing happened.

I pulled again, harder, and this time the lucáfu turned her head and chittered at me angrily.

"Well, all right then, how do I do it?" I thought to her. "I'm new at this. You have to help me."

She turned her green eyes on mine, and a picture formed in my mind: a hand closing around the base of the teat and squeezing gently down to the tip. I tried it that way, and a few drops of yellow milk emerged. On the second squeeze I got more, and soon the milk was flowing freely.

By the time I finished with all six teats, my hands were cramping. And there was the other lucáfu still to be milked. I shook my hands out, rubbed them a bit, then said to the second beast, "Come on, then. I'll do my best."

The animal only looked at me and shook its head, chittering.

"What's the matter? Don't you want to be milked? I'm sure you need it." The second lucáfu turned and began to walk away.

I huffed. Weren't Falendan animals supposed to be cooperative? What about that great friendship between man and beast Meli kept talking about?

I went after the lucáfu. "Get on up there, mate. It's milking time and you know it." The animal kept walking—in the wrong direction.

I caught up to it and pushed it around to face the platform. "Don't make me get tough with you."

The lucáfu looked at me with an expression in its large brown eyes that reminded me of the maths master when I divided two by two and got zero. It made a sound like a sigh, turned, and mounted the platform.

"That's more like it." I sat on the stool, parted the long wool, and reached for the animal's udder.

Then I pulled back my hand in a hurry. Apparently this lucáfu was a male.

I covered my face with my hands. What an idiot. I really couldn't do anything right.

Something nudged my arm. I looked up through my fingers to see the lucáfu butting gently against me and chittering in a low, soft way that sounded an awful lot like laughter. It even seemed to be smiling.

I dropped my hands. All the animals in the yard were looking at me, each making a breathy, staccato version of its own call. They were all laughing at me. But the funny thing was, I didn't mind. I threw an arm over the lucáfu's neck and laughed along with them.

I was hungry enough to eat hay with the animals when Marala finally called me inside. "I have done what I can for Meli," she told me. "I have bathed her leg in calivóda and given her the juice of the red lenafálina to drink. The green is only for surface healing; red is needed for bones. But it will take some hours to rebuild the bone. We will eat, and then she must rest."

Meli was sitting up on her pallet, the lavender color back in her cheeks, looking almost her usual self. I felt a weight lift from my heart at the sight of her.

We lunched on fruit and cheese, and I told them about my milking adventure. Meli laughed so hard she almost fell off her pallet.

"Well, you can't blame me. In my world it's easy to tell males and females apart. How was I supposed to know?"

Meli apologized and controlled herself with an effort. Marala only smiled. "You will learn the ways of our animals in time. You can tell the male lucáfu by the color of its eyes. The females have green eyes, and the males have brown. It is the same with the balikuni."

Okay, yeah, I'd noticed Nila's eyes were green. "There's so much to learn. If I can't get a simple thing like milking right— how will I ever succeed in destroying the Dome?"

"Do not worry, Danny. The knowledge will come to you as you need it. And you will not be alone. No True Falendan is ever alone—and you are becoming one of us now."

AFTER LUNCH MARALA DREW A CURTAIN around Meli's pallet. "She must rest." Then she pulled a basket from a niche in the rock. "Come outside, and I will show you the history of our world."

I followed her, puzzled. The basket held a bunch of crystalline sheets. How could Marala "show" me their history with those?

We sat on a rock bench, and she pulled one of the sheets from the basket. It glinted pale violet in the sun.

"This is the violet lenafálina. It grows differently from the others, in flat slabs like this. Its power is to preserve thoughts so that they may be passed down through time or across long distances. When a sheet of violet lenafálina has been filled with thoughts, we call it a likúmena."

"Oh—you mean—sort of like a book?"

"What is this thing you call 'book'?"

"It's a bunch of pieces of paper, kind of stuck together on one side, with writing on them."

Marala shook her head. "Paper . . . writing . . . I think it will be easier if I simply search your mind. May I?"

Marala was the first Falendan to ask permission to examine the inside of my head. Meli had grown up without her parents—maybe she never learned proper manners. "Sure, go ahead."

She fastened her eyes on mine for a minute, her nousíniki waving toward me, then said, "Ah, I see. Yes, I think a book serves somewhat the same purpose as our violet lenafálina, although the form is very different. But you seem to have a great many books in your world. In your mind I see

111

whole buildings full of them. I suppose it is because that is the only way you can share your thoughts with each other. But you make your books out of dead trees! What a pity that so many trees must die just so that you can communicate. With us it is much simpler."

She put the crystalline sheet in my hands. "You need only hold the likúmena and bend your thought toward it, and you will hear it just as you hear my thoughts. But you will perceive images as well—even odors, tastes, and textures. It is like partaking of another's experience."

I held the sheet and concentrated on it. At first I thought it wasn't working properly. My mind was filled with vague shadowy shapes and swirls of mist. Could you get bad reception with these things, like on a television set, if you weren't very good at thought-reading?

But then the familiar sort of echo-voice began to speak. "In the beginning, the Great One created Falenda out of the mists of time and the abundance of his grace."

The shadowy shapes and wraiths of mist resolved into a planet ringed with clouds. As the clouds parted, swathes of violet, orange, and deep blue spread across the planet's surface, bounded by large areas of pale green that I took for seas. A heavenly scent surrounded me, as if I were smelling all the flowers ever created at once. I could hardly believe it. I was witnessing the making of a world.

As the voice went on I saw, in fast forward, everything it described. "He was helped in his work of creation by the elúndina, his faithful servants." The familiar winged creatures flew about over the face of the planet, but their wings were much larger than the elúndina I'd seen before—bigger even than when they attacked the nikhi in the meadow. They looked more like flamingo wings than butterflies, but much larger even than that.

"But one of them was not so faithful. One was jealous and wished to possess Falenda for his own. His name was Elífalu, and he was the most splendid of all the elúndina. His wings shimmered with colors beyond the rainbow, and when he spread them he could gather all the light of the sun. The Great One loved Elífalu and had planned to place Falenda under his protection; but Elífalu was proud, and he chose to grab what the Great One would have freely offered.

"Elífalu, the darling of the elúndina, easily persuaded others of his brethren to follow him. His light dazzled them so that they could not see the ultimate light of the Great One. They formed an army and warred against the Great One and the elúndina who remained faithful to Him."

Now gigantic iridescent wings flapped and crashed over the whole surface of the planet. At first I could hardly tell the difference between them; but gradually, some of them darkened into twilight. Then the iridescent wings got the upper hand, and the twilight wings closed ranks over one area of the surface.

"As he saw his defeat approaching, Elífalu sought to destroy the world he could not own. His fury scorched and withered a tenth part of all the ground." The twilight wings, now almost black, swooped close to the surface and burned everything they passed. The smoke of a smoldering forest fire filled my lungs. Then, just as I thought I was going to choke, the smoke faded. Iridescent wings covered the devastated land.

"At last the Great One and his armies were victorious. Elífalu and his followers were banished from the light and became darkness. The scorched ground was raised up into mountains, and deep under those mountains Elífalu and his minions were buried. But he was no longer called Elífalu. The Great One renamed him Hakagrug, the Destroyer."

With that the likúmena showed me a scene much like what I'd seen last afternoon, as Meli and I drew near the mountains—only everything was sharper and more vivid. The world as it was now looked like a faded photograph in comparison.

"The Great One then created the Falendan race to rule the land, with a few of his elúndina to guard them; but the elúndina that remained diminished in size and power so the Falendan race could flourish. The armies of Hakagrug, imprisoned with him under the mountains, became the nikhi, and Hakagrug bided his time until he could take his revenge."

Marala took the likúmena from my hands. "The rest of the story you already know. If we are not victorious, Hakagrug's revenge will soon be complete."

CHAPTER SEVENTEEN

In Which I Look Like a Weakling

MARALA WOKE ME BEFORE DAWN next morning. Meli was already up and walking around, with no trace of a limp. She turned to smile at me, and my heart did a jumping jack.

"I'm—glad you're better," I said, stumbling over the words.

She must know everything that was in my mind—even the things I didn't understand myself yet. But her thought-answer was only, "Thank you, Danny. You saved my life—and restored me to my mother. My debt to you is great."

"No debt," I mumbled. "Just did what had to be done."

"Nevertheless, you did it bravely and cleverly, and with true friendship. I am grateful."

I could have floated to the top of the mountain in two seconds flat.

We changed into new clothes Marala gave us—short tunics with leggings tucked into stout leather boots. I thanked the Great One I wouldn't have to climb a mountain in those sandals. My things fit me pretty well, considering, but Meli's looked like they'd been made for her. Amazing someone so slender could still have all the right curves.

We loaded small packs with a few necessities. Then Marala brought out two lengths of lightweight cloth and handed one of them to Meli. Marala wrapped hers around her nousíniki in two seconds flat, but Meli fumbled, ending up with a gourd-like lump that fell over one eye and left a gaping hole at the back. I hid my smile with my hand, but she knew she looked ridiculous.

Her lavender skin flushed deep purple. "I have never worn a turban before. There seems to be some trick to it."

Marala unwound Meli's tangle and rewrapped it. "You will learn, my daughter. We must wear these always—until the Dome is destroyed."

We sat down to breakfast. I ate like it was my last meal, only wishing for a nice hot cup of tea to take the edge off the morning's chill. Then Marala set a cup of steaming liquid by my plate.

"What's this?"

"Calivóda," she answered. "It is for drinking as well as bathing. It will give you strength."

It actually smelled a bit like tea, and the taste was close enough I could pretend. But the effect was like that of the calivóda bath. I felt as if I could climb a hundred mountains before lunch.

By midday, though, I figured I'd be lucky to climb one mountain in about a week. The rock face was just short of perpendicular, so for each step I had to find handholds and footholds and hoist myself up with all four limbs. My cloak kept getting caught on an elbow or wrapped around a knee, but I needed it for protection against the icy wind that roared down from the mountaintop without pausing for breath.

My training on the bell tower helped me out for the first leg
of the climb, but I was a sprinter; I'd never needed this kind of
endurance. Marala, who must be pushing forty in Earth years,

and Meli, with her newly mended leg, practically leapt up the mountainside ahead of me, only pausing to let me catch my breath.

"What is it?" I asked them in thought-speech as we rested on a ledge. I had no wind to spare for conversation. "Is it the air? The melikunápitu? What makes you so strong?"

Mother and daughter looked at each other. "It is simply the way we are," Meli said at last. "We have been wondering what makes you so weak."

I picked a rock from the sole of my boot. "Well, I don't climb mountains every day, you know. We Earthlings have to train for this kind of thing. It doesn't come naturally."

Marala sent me a thought that felt like what I remembered of my mother's touch. "Perhaps it is because your race as a whole is Flattened. When we wish to climb or jump, we simply make ourselves buoyant." She gazed at me for a moment and I felt her thought probing my mind. "It seems this concept is foreign to you?"

"I'll say!" I stared at her. "How on earth—I mean how do you do that? I don't see anything different about you—no inflatable air bladders or anything." I pictured a puffer fish.

Meli laughed her chiming laugh. "How silly you are, Danny! What would we look like all puffed up with air? No, it is our nousíniki that make us buoyant."

"Your nousíniki! No, really, that's too much. You mean you can *fly* with those things?"

"Not fly, no, or we would simply fly up the mountain and carry you with us. We can only become a little lighter for a time."

"But how does it work? Is something weird going on under those turbans? It doesn't make sense."

Marala smiled. "Many things in Falenda do not 'make sense' by the standards of your world, Danny. Can people there communicate with their thoughts or create light with their hair? Yet you have accepted that these things are real."

"Do you remember when we first met?" Meli broke in. "You wondered if our world had more than three dimensions. In a sense it does, but the other dimension is not physical. Our nousíniki operate in that other dimension, although they exist in the three you can see and feel."

I shook my head. "There are more things in heaven and Earth, Horatio, than are dreamt of in your philosophy," I mumbled to myself.

As we continued up the cliff, the cold wind took on a new dimension of its own: a nauseating odor, like a warm room shut up for days with something decaying inside. That stale stink being carried on a furious icy gale bothered my mind as much as my nose—it just didn't fit. I shot a thought up to Marala: "What's that horrid smell?"

"That is the smell of evil, the smell of Flattening. The smell of Hakagrug. I am afraid you must get used to it, Danny; it will only get worse from now on."

As soon as I had a stable foothold, I rummaged in my belt pouch for a handkerchief and tied it over my nose and mouth. The handkerchief wasn't any too fresh, but it helped a little. When I was small, I played at bandits with a kerchief my mother tied for me that way. She acted the helpless victim I captured and tied to the railroad tracks (a ladder laid on the kitchen floor). Then I would rip off the kerchief and become the hero who untied her in the nick of time, before the train came barreling down.

I knew better than to look down, but so far I hadn't looked

up any farther than my next handhold. Now I held tight to the rock and craned my neck back, hoping to catch a glimpse of the cliff top. But the jagged rock stretched away above me. And the day was more than half gone.

"We must keep moving," came Marala's thought-voice. "We must reach the top by sunset. There is no place to rest along the cliff, and the nikhi will be out in force tonight. There is a farming village near the edge. We must reach shelter there before it is fully dark."

I adjusted my pack. Already my muscles felt like lead. "Too bad your nousíniki can't lift *me* a little," I grumbled.

Meli and Marala paused above me and exchanged glances. "Perhaps we can help after all," Marala said. She took off her pack and pulled out a deep blue rope, made, I supposed, from the tílamel vines that surrounded her clearing. She handed one end to Meli and tossed the center of the rope to me. "Loop this around your waist," she told me.

When the three of us were securely tied, we climbed on. I couldn't feel the rope pulling me, but each step was easier than before. I caught up to them right away and kept up so well I began to feel a little proud of myself—till I remembered it was all because of the rope.

Even so, the sky's gold was fading to grey and my limbs felt like jelly when we reached the top. I planted my feet on horizontal soil and doubled over, lungs heaving, only to gag on the stale, disgusting air of Hakagrug. Marala gazed at me with compassion.

"I know you are weary, Danny, but we must not rest here; it is not safe in the twilight. We must get to shelter." She pointed across a flat expanse of gravel and dried grasses to what looked like a clump of rocks in the distance. "It is a farming village where the people are friendly to our cause. Come now, we must go quickly."

I took the rope off my waist, readjusted my handkerchief and my pack, and trudged off behind Marala.

Meli fell back to walk beside me. "I am also weary, Danny, and there is pain in my leg."

I saw she was limping slightly. What a git I was—I'd been feeling sorry for myself, when it was Meli who was really suffering.

"I—I could carry you. Piggy-back. At least I think I could." I didn't really think I could, but it seemed the gentlemanly thing to offer.

She smiled. "It is kind of you, but I think we will progress faster this way. The pain is not so very bad. If I could, perhaps, lean on your arm?"

"Sure thing." I stuck out my elbow and she took it, with a pressure I could hardly feel; but it was enough to ease her limp.

Somehow her hand on my arm gave me new energy. We hurried to catch up with Marala. The clump of rock soon rose against the greying sky and turned into a cluster of low stone cottages with thatched roofs, surrounded by violet fields with multicolored orchards beyond. It was the closest thing to an English village I'd seen in Falenda. I felt better just looking at it.

The last light was fading as we reached the nearest cottage. Marala stopped in front of the door. She didn't lift a hand to knock, but a tall Falendan man swung open the door and shooed us inside.

"Quickly," his thought-voice said. "The nikhi are abroad."

CHAPTER EIGHTEEN

In Which I Become a Citizen

THE MAN INTRODUCED HIMSELF AS Túlamen and his wife as Ruávena. They both bowed toward me. "Welcome, Deliverer, to our home. We have little with which to honor you, but all that we have is yours."

I bowed back. You'd think I'd be used to this kind of thing by now, but I wasn't. "Thanks, but all we need is a meal and a bed."

Ruávena waved her hand at a small, low table spread with a typical Falendan meal. The fruits were kind of shriveled and pale compared to the ones in the valley.

"Our food is but poor here, compared with the lowlands," Túlamen said. "The evil air stunts the trees." He began a blessing song in Falendan, and the others joined in. Before I could get my wits about me and attempt my own harmony, the song was over.

As we ate, Marala pumped Tulamen for updates about what had happened in the City in the last seven years.

Tulamen shook his head. "It is much worse now. I know of

none who have escaped complete Flattening. The spies have increased, and so has the guard on the Tower. To gain entrance and climb the Tower will take most of the day. We will have no time to gather a choir, even if there were singers to be found."

"We?" I thought to him. "Are you coming with us?"

"Of course. You must have a farmer with you to get through the City gates. And Ruávena will come as well."

"What about the rest of the village? If we need more singers, couldn't they come too?"

"A large group would be too conspicuous. One or two families may travel together, but not more."

"What if we split up? The five of us could go together, and others could follow a little later."

Tulamen considered. "If they left much later, they would not reach the City before the gates close at sunset. But perhaps we can find a way. In the morning we will ask the others."

AT FIRST LIGHT, MARALA AND TULAMEN went out and returned with some other villagers. They all gathered around the table, and I counted seven new faces—four men and three women. Tulamen introduced them all, but there was no way I could remember all those names, or even tell them apart. You don't realize how much you rely on things like height, build, and coloring to identify people until you're confronted with a bunch of people who have all those things in common. I had to be around them for awhile before I could see the subtle differences in their features.

Tulamen began a song, which I figured was a sort of morning prayer. This time I managed to join in, and the song modulated around my voice. I closed my eyes and let the music flow from a deep place inside me. What came out was the most beautiful, praiseful melody I'd ever heard. The final chord rang within that little cottage almost as if I were back in the cathedral.

When I opened my eyes, all the Falendans were looking at me with an expression between amazement and reverence. I wasn't ready for that.

Tulamen spoke, as if for them all: "You are a great singer, Danny. You were not born to our song, and yet you were able to lead it to a new and most beautiful conclusion. Now we know that you are indeed the Deliverer we have awaited so long."

I didn't know whether to shout for joy or climb in a hole and pull it in after me. For the first time I could almost believe I might really be able to do what I'd been sent to do. But there was so little time . . .

"Shouldn't we get started?" I asked.

Tulamen bowed. "We await only your word."

That floored me. Me, the leader of an expedition? I didn't have a clue. "Uh . . . Well . . . We have to split up, right? So should Meli and Marala and I go first? Oh, wait, you said we have to have a farmer with us, so I suppose that means Tulamen and Ruávena too. Is that too many at once?"

Tulamen answered, "I think if we make two groups of six, we may pass unregarded. Perhaps one of the men could come with us. Lóravel?" The youngest-looking of the men nodded.

We worked out that the second group would follow us after an hour or so and spend the night in another village closer to the City. Our group would stay at a farmers' inn on the main avenue, and we would all meet up the next morning at the Tower of Grozlukh. We might have been planning a holiday at Brighton.

Now we had to disguise ourselves. Marala had her own

eye-shields from before, and one of the men had a pair to fit Meli. For me it was a little more complicated.

Tulamen handed me a jar full of thick gray glop. "Garama juice. Ordinarily we use it to dye the cloth that we sell in the City. Today we will use it to dye your skin."

The women went out to load the cart. I took off my tunic, and Tulamen smeared my back with the juice. It went on like sun lotion but absorbed quickly, leaving my skin a sickly-looking light purplish gray.

Tulamen handed the jar to me, along with a tunic of the same dull gray, and went out. I smeared the lotion on the rest of me, hoping I'd covered my face evenly. Falendan homes didn't have mirrors. Then I put on the gray tunic and went out to join the others. They were clustered about a small cart loaded with bushels of anemic fruit and bales of dyed gray cloth.

Meli was just putting on her eye-shields. She turned to look at me, and we both froze in shock. Other Falendans looked fine with blue eyes, but on Meli they were wrong, and a little scary.

She stared at me open-mouthed. "You look like a Flattened One," she said in a horrified thought-whisper.

"Well, that is the idea, isn't it?" Why did she have to look at me like that?

"I suppose so, but . . ." She looked away. "It frightens me."

Marala turned her blue-shielded eyes on the two of us. The blue didn't bother me as much on her. "This is but a tiny fore-taste. Many things will frighten us all in the days to come."

She had to mention that, when I'd managed to forget it for a second. Before nightfall, if all went well, I'd be in the City—which I'd begun thinking of as the City of Doom. And tomorrow I'd have to accomplish the impossible. If my skin hadn't been dyed gray, I'd have been as pale as a ghost.

125

"We must take courage," Marala said. "The Great One has called us to this task, and he will not fail us." I sure hoped she was right about that. "Come. It is time we were off."

THE CART WAS PULLED BY A BALIKUNI—a thin and watery-eyed one with a grayish coat—but we all had to travel on foot. The terrain was different up here—flat like the lowlands, but except for the fields around the village, the soil was rocky and bare. Sharp stones poked their corners through my boot soles and into my feet, still tender from yesterday's climb. The air was frigid, but close and oppressive, and the horrible stench got stronger every minute. The handkerchief was useless against it, but I kept it on anyway. The golden light, warm and comforting in the lowlands, was harsh and glaring up here. I hoped the garama juice would act as a kind of sunscreen; otherwise my fair skin would be beet-red by evening. *What's blond and gray and red all over? A sunburned Earthling.* As a joke it lacked that certain zing.

As soon as we left the village, I glimpsed a shape on the horizon. That is, I saw not so much the shape itself as the light glinting off it. "Is that the City?" I asked Marala.

"That is the Dome, yes."

As we went on, the shape of the Dome grew clearer, and

126

the light reflecting from it splintered into all the colors of the spectrum. "But—it's beautiful!"

Marala turned grave eyes on me. "Do not let its beauty blind you. It is a prison. On the inside it is covered with soot and grime. There is so little light there that they have to produce it artificially, even in the day. Think of it, Danny—thousands of people passing their lives without ever seeing the light of the sun."

A memory came to me of a rare sunny day in West Sussex, a picnic in the countryside, my mother running, laughing, dancing with me in the warm yellow light. Mum had almost worshiped the sun—and now she had lived seven years without a glimpse of it. If, that is, she was still alive.

In the late afternoon we came opposite a cluster of cottages, about half a mile away, surrounded by violet fields that came up to border our path. "That is the village where the second group will spend the night," Tulamen said.

"Shall I go there and warn them the others are coming?" Loravel asked. "Perhaps I could recruit more singers as well."

I glanced from Marala to Tulamen, waiting for them to respond to this suggestion. But they were all looking expectantly at me. Oh, right, I was supposed to be the leader.

"That sounds like a good idea," I said, fingers crossed that it really was.

We all said goodbye to Loravel, a bit choked up—Ruávena and Tulamen especially. The chance was in all our minds that we might not see him again. He set off at a steady lope. We watched his retreating figure for a while, then set our faces toward the City.

The Dome now loomed before us, filling my field of vision, taking over my mind. It was unimaginably huge, like a manmade mountain. The sheer size of it shriveled my newly budded confidence like a fallen leaf. The light reflecting off it nearly blinded me.

From this distance I could make out separate crystalline panes, each of a different color. "Are all these different kinds of lenafálina?" I asked Meli. "I've seen green and red for healing, violet for likúmena, blue for eyesight, gold for the mind. But there must be hundreds of colors there."

She nodded. "The variety is nearly infinite. Only a relative few have properties that are known to us; the others are rare and were not discovered until the Highlanders began to dig deep into the chasm. But those that make up the Dome are dead and have no power but to contain and amplify the evil within."

As we came near the Dome, we saw other parties approaching from different directions, most, like us, with laden carts. "It is time for you to conceal yourself, Danny," said Tulamen. "You must not be seen outside the City, for it is not permitted for the Flattened Ones to go outside the gates without a passport."

We stopped, and the others moved aside bolts of cloth so I could crawl underneath. Tulamen restacked the bolts so their weight was taken by the baskets on either side. I had an airhole through which I could see a little, but all there was to see at this point was the sky.

"Your body is hidden, Danny," Marala's thought-voice said, "but you must also strive to conceal your thoughts. At the gate there will no doubt be spies who are able to read thoughts, and they will detect your presence if you do not cloak your mind."

I tamped down a seed of panic. "But how do I do that?"

"It is a skill we all learn from childhood; there is no time to teach you our way. But I believe if you anchor your thoughts within your own world, they will be incomprehensible to any spies. You must think very hard of your own world, Danny, and on no account send out a thought toward any of us, nor allow our images into your mind. It will be best if you begin now, and do not stop until we release you from hiding."

Of everything I'd had to do on Falenda so far, this seemed the hardest: to harness my thoughts and keep them pointed in a single direction. Yet so much depended on it.

Then Meli's face appeared above my peephole. "Goodbye, Danny. I will be here beside you, but I must not think of you any more than you must think of me." That was the greatest separation possible. She gave me a pale smile, and I reached out to her with a last thought; then she was gone.

I turned my thoughts inward. How many times had I sat in class, my mind worlds away while the master droned on about history or science or maths. Then I'd dreamed of other universes, in which my family was whole again and Bull and his cronies were light-years away. Now I had to turn those daydreams inside out.

I'd have to focus on the few pleasant things about my old life. Any strong emotion would give me away. Thoughts of singing weren't safe either; my voice was my concealed weapon. What was left? Stargazing with Mum from the bell tower. Mentally I traveled over the night sky, through every constellation I could remember and the stories from Greek mythology Mum had told me about each one. Orion, the great hunter, chasing the Pleiades nymphs across the sky with his dog, Canis. Cassiopeia, who bragged about her daughter's beauty and was condemned by Venus to hang upside down forever. Ursa Major, a princess unlucky enough to attract

Zeus's attention, so jealous Hera turned her into the Great Bear.

I hoped the Falendan Great One was more like the God of my cathedral than those petty old pagan ones, or I could end up in the sky right along with them for having the hubris to attempt this mission. But I mustn't think about that.

By the time I got through the constellations, I could hear creaking cartwheels, honking balikuni, and tinkling Falendan voices all around me. We must be near the gates. Quickly, back to Earth—how about my favorite telly programmes? *Doctor Who*—no, too dangerous, all those other worlds. Books, then—but my favorite books were all other-world fantasies too. Maybe *The Hobbit* would be safe. I lost myself with a smile in Bilbo's unexpected tea party.

The noise and confusion got louder. It was all I could do to focus on Bilbo. The cart jolted wildly, and the bolts threatened to slide off me—I thought of Bilbo tumbling downstream in a barrel. I heard loud, harsh voices, crescendoing to a cry, and zoomed in on the shouting goblin soldiers cringing from Gandalf's elf-hewn sword.

The cart jounced and rumbled over what felt like cobblestones and finally came to rest. The noise had diminished from fortissimo to mezzo forte.

I held my breath, as if that would help me hold back my thoughts. A bolt of cloth slid back, and before I had time to panic, Meli's face appeared in the gap. "Quickly, Danny! They've taken my mother and the others!"

CHAPTER NINETEEN

In Which Meli Learns to Improvise

I SCRAMBLED OUT OF THE CART, tossing bolts of cloth and tipping fruit from bushels to roll across the cobblestones. "What happened? Did I give us away?"

She shook her head. "I do not think any of us did. There was no time. As soon as we reached the gate, the guards grabbed them. I was behind the cart and had a moment to make myself unnoticeable—a gift we logosagamis have, as my mother mentioned before. Fortunately they were not interested in the cart. I waited until they had all gone, then brought you here."

I looked around. I might almost have been in one of the dirtier parts of London. Windowless stone walls rose on either side of a narrow alleyway, so high I couldn't see their tops. I couldn't see the sky, either, only a lighter patch of gray. Small brownish-gray animals rooted in the garbage that lined the walls. The stench was so fierce I almost puked.

Meli covered her face with her hands. "This is a terrible place, Danny. The moment we entered, the guards seized the others. And I could not follow them, not even with my thoughts—I would have given myself away, and then there would be no one to help you."

She looked at me so piteously I wanted to hug her, comfort her. But I had no idea what a hug would mean to a Falendan. It might be offensive—or it might be a marriage proposal.

"What do you think tipped the guards off?"

"I do not know. Perhaps someone betrayed us. You do not think—it could have been Loravel?"

"No. I'm sure Tulamen trusted him, and I trust Tulamen. But there could've been nikhi in that other village. They could've overheard him and warned the guards." I shrugged. "Doesn't matter. We've just got to rescue them. You see which way they went?"

"Straight down the main street. But then I lost sight of them." Her eyes stood out large in a face stretched tight over her fine bones. "Oh, Danny—even with the turban, I can barely hear you for the Noise."

"Noise?" I heard wagon wheels and animals and voices, muffled by the walls of the alleyway—nothing to the everyday noise of Midchester.

She stared at me. "Don't you hear it? In your head— 'Sale on finest quality jewel-encrusted toothpicks . . . Increase your mining quota by twenty percent . . . possess this ultimate status symbol.' It hasn't stopped since we entered the City. If I stay here long I'll go mad."

I focused inward and could sense another level of noise in my mind—a babble of Falendan voices. The tone went from sharp and insistent, to wheedling and seductive, to bright with a forced gaiety. Like adverts on the telly back home—it got into my nervous system and made me unsettled and jumpy. In the deep quiet of the lowlands of Falenda, I'd felt a kind of peace. I wasn't aware of it until it was gone.

"I hear it, but I can't understand the words. When you thought-speak to me, it comes through like English; but this stuff is untranslated Falendan."

"The voices are not speaking directly to you. It is fortunate for you that you do not understand. All is greed, ambition, cloying pleasures, false promises—oh, my people, my people!" Her anguish was a knife in my gut.

Time to move. "If we go back near the gate, perhaps we'll hear people talking, pick up some clues." Meli started after me, moving like a robot, her eyes dull. "I think we'd better bring the cart, don't you? It's your cover."

She stopped, nodded dumbly, and reached back to take the balikuni's reins. Then for a second her eyes took on their old sparkle. "And you had better take off that handkerchief. The Flattened Ones are accustomed to the smell."

I yanked it off and shoved it in my belt-pouch. "Can you lead the way back to the gate?"

She nodded and set off. I followed a few paces behind the cart, trying to look as if I belonged there. The streets were full of people, all walking quickly with their heads down, not meeting each other's eyes. I kept my head down as far as I could while still taking in the streets around me. I'd have to find my own way if Meli was overcome by the Noise.

After a couple of blocks, though, I gave up on orienting myself by sight. Every block looked the same: solid cliffs of stone on either side, punctuated by identical gray wooden doors. Signs hung on some of the buildings, but if those spiky symbols were writing, they meant nothing to me.

It wasn't long before we reached the square just inside the gates. Meli hung back. "What if someone recognizes me?"

"Well, they won't recognize me." I strode out into the crowd. People were gesturing excitedly toward the gate and down the broad avenue, talking aloud in voices like clanging brass instead of the tinkling crystal I was used to. I wondered if even Meli would understand them.

I went back to her. "You'll have to come with me. I can't tell what they're saying."

A spasm crossed her face, but she nodded. The square was too packed for the cart to move, so she tied the balikuni to a post and sidled into the crowd.

A few minutes later she came back and stood at the other side of the cart. Not looking at me, she thought, "A man and two women were taken to the dungeon. It is right in the center of the city—beneath the Tower of Grozlukh."

I reeled. The prison was underneath the very Tower we'd have to climb to sing down the Dome. The Tower Tulamen had told us was now so well guarded. My mother and Meli's father must be there too. I'd been counting on Marala and Tulamen to get us past the guards. Now Meli and I would have to get in on our own, rescue all the adults, and still reach the top by nightfall.

At least, though, we knew where we had to go. Far in the distance, at the end of the wide main street, a tall black needle pierced the murk. "Come on," I thought to Meli and pushed my way forward through the crowd.

Not that I enjoyed being elbow-to-elbow with these people. The City-dwellers looked pathetic and revolting. Their skin, the same gray as mine, was dry and almost scaly. From every head grew what looked like ordinary, dirty-blond hair. The most disturbing thing was their eyes. They had no color at all and no life behind them. They were like windows into an empty room.

134

But if the Citizens themselves were like clones of one drab creature, their clothing and hair made up for it. They made the styles on the fashion-mag covers back home look normal. I could hardly tell the men from the women—all were decked out with braids, loops, and curls, drapes, sashes, and sleeves, so complex I wondered how these people ever managed to dress themselves or move. And yet everything was that same drab gray.

The ground under my feet trembled. Did they have earthquakes here? I looked around for Meli and noticed a gaping doorway into a small room packed with people. As one body they exited—all men, dressed in plain tunics and round gray helmets like hard hats. An identical group took their place, and the doors closed. A lift! The lenafálina mines were directly under the city. They must be blasting down there—cutting through miles of rock, ever closer to Hakagrug's prison.

I plunged forward again. The street was so crowded I was afraid the cart might not be able to get through. But Meli kept close behind me, and the crowd thinned as people turned off into doorways. Over the general stench I caught an odor I hadn't smelled since I arrived in Falenda—roasting meat. My mind, conditioned to Falendan ways, revolted at the thought, but my stomach responded to the smell with a growl. It was dinnertime. We hadn't eaten for hours.

I stopped and waited for Meli, then thought to her, "It's getting late. We need to find that inn Tulamen talked about so we can eat. And we'll have to leave the balikuni and cart there too. We can't take them with us to the Tower."

"True. And if we left them on the street, they would be stolen—and possibly even—" Meli shuddered, and I knew she meant the animal might become someone's dinner. "And we ourselves must not be out after dark. The curfew here is strictly enforced."

She looked around at the building signs, which all looked alike to me, and pointed to one a short way down on the opposite side. The sign hung over an open gateway large enough for a cart to go through. "There, that must be it."

We made for the inn, but I stopped outside the gate. "What about money?"

Meli's silver eyebrows drew together. "I have none, for we do not use it in the Lowlands. But we have the goods in the cart. Perhaps the innkeeper will accept a bushel of fruit in exchange for our dinner and lodging."

"Right. You'd better handle that, since you're supposed to be the farmer. Not to mention I can't talk to these people."

"But how are we to account for our being together?"

I shrugged. "We could be doing business together. I could be negotiating to buy your cloth." It wouldn't fly in twenty-first-century England, but in Falenda kids our age acted pretty much like adults.

She chewed her bottom lip. "I do not like this deception. It is not the True Falendan way."

No, and I shuddered to think what a poor liar Meli would make. We'd have to rely on the City-dwellers being as unperceptive as they looked.

I hated lying almost as much as Meli did. "We have a saying in my world: 'Be wise as serpents but gentle as doves.' I think it's time for us to be wise as serpents."

"Wise as—what? What does that mean?"

"It means—well, if you're dealing with a crafty enemy, sometimes you have to be crafty too. But you never forget which side you're on. You don't let them bring you down to their level."

136

Meli nodded, thoughtful. "I see. Yes, there is wisdom in that." She glanced over my shoulder. "And I think we should begin now, because a woman over there is staring at us. No, do not turn around. Let us go in."

I followed her through the wide gateway into an open courtyard, where a number of turbaned True Falendans were milling about among the City-dwellers. I was relieved to see many of them haggling over prices—coins changed hands and goods were lifted from carts. Maybe Meli and I would blend in after all.

While Meli went in search of the innkeeper, I stood by our cart and got my bearings. One side of the courtyard was divided into large stalls, most of which held a balikuni and cart. From the rear building people came and went with baskets and platters of food; that must be the kitchen. The door on the third side stood open, with light, voices, and the clatter of serving streaming out: the dining room, where Meli had gone.

In the corner between the dining room and the kitchen I noticed one woman, a City-dweller, standing alone. I got the feeling she'd been watching me but had just looked away. Was that the same woman Meli had seen outside?

I knew I ought to ignore her, but something about her held my gaze. She was short for a Falendan, not much taller than me. She wore a plain, long, belted gown, and her single braid was wrapped closely around her head. That alone set her apart. But her eyes—that was what really struck me—her eyes weren't colorless and empty like all the others. In fact—but no, that was impossible, a trick of the light from this distance. I'd thought for a second her eyes had whites to them, which no Falendan's eyes ever had.

Meli came back, a stout Citizen following her. His tunic was belted into three huge puffs, then cropped short above flabby knees. His hair stood out almost like unflattened nousíniki. But on second glance I saw it had been braided around stiff wires into a bunch of tiny plaits. He and Meli spoke, his brassy City accent garish against her tinkling voice. Then he chose two bushels of fruit (the best two), clapped his hands, and a couple of boys appeared from the kitchen to carry them. A third boy materialized from the stable and led our balikuni inside.

The innkeeper motioned for Meli and me to follow him into the dining room. Out of the corner of my eye, I saw the strange woman leave her corner to come after us.

"Meli, that woman you saw outside—I think she followed us in here. There's something funny about her. She's not like the rest of them."

"I know. We must be very careful. She could be a friend—or a spy. Try not to thought-speak to me any more than you have to, just in case."

The innkeeper led us to a small table in a corner. We sat facing into the room, but the woman, if she had really followed us, faded into the crowd. A girl brought us a platter full of dishes I didn't recognize, but some of them smelled like roasted meat. Meli spoke to the girl, and with a scornful look she took half the dishes back again. We were left with a modest meal and two tall mugs of brown liquid. I looked around for the strange woman before digging in, but saw no sign of her.

Meli sniffed at her mug and made a face. I took a cautious sip from mine. The taste was unfamiliar, but the way it felt going down my throat reminded me of the beer my father used to let me have on special occasions, before Mum disappeared.

I left it alone after that. I knew too well what too much beer could do.

We both attacked the food voraciously. I was working on a huge mouthful of bread and cheese when I heard my name. I turned to Meli, then realized someone had spoken aloud—with a British accent. I looked up sharply to see the woman from the courtyard.

"May I sit down?" she said in English, and then she smiled. And with the smile I knew her.

The strange woman with the un-Falendan eyes was Celia Cutler—my mother.

CHAPTER TWENTY

In Which I Find a Treasure and Lose It Again

FELT AS IF THE BLASTING that shivered the ground beneath us every few minutes had jolted everything inside me out of its normal place. To see my mother again after all these years—I should be leaping, dancing, screaming with joy, squeezing her until she gasped out, laughing, as she used to do when I was small, "Danny, I'm not your teddy bear. I need to breathe!"

But I did none of these things.

I told myself it was only the situation that stopped me. The last thing we wanted was to call attention to ourselves. And yet...

"M—mother?" I gasped. "What—how—Marala said you'd been captured. We thought you'd be in prison!" *And why are you not surprised to see me?* I thought but didn't say.

She sat down on the bench, beside me but not touching me. "I was—until today. When they brought in Marala and those others, there was some confusion and I was able to escape."

"What is she saying?" Meli thought to me insistently. "Her mind is closed. I cannot hear her thoughts."

I translated.

Meli's face filled with consternation. "Then what of my father? Was he not imprisoned with her? Did he not escape as well? Why is she alone?"

"Mother," I said, "this is Meli. Marala and Falakúr's daughter. She wants to know what happened to her father. Why were you the only one who escaped?"

My mother spoke to Meli, and I repeated her words in my thoughts. "Falakúr and I were kept separate all these years. I don't really know what's become of him. I'm sorry, dear. But I can tell you the prison was not as horrible as you might think. More like a hotel, really, except of course one couldn't leave. I'd expect your father to be as well as I am." She smiled.

Truly, she looked as though she'd been staying at a posh resort—clean, well dressed, well fed, content. Like a pampered cat. Not bursting with joy at recovering her long-lost son, not wary from years of anxious self-preservation, not jumpy with fear of capture. Just content.

She turned to me again. "Look at you, all grown up. Are you in the choir school, as we planned?"

I nodded. The choir school seemed like a dream to me now.

"And your father? How is he?"

"Not—not so good. He really misses you. And he drinks—a lot. He's lost his job. He says we may have to move."

A shadow crossed her face, and she touched her fingers to my cheek. But it wasn't the soft touch I remembered. Each fingertip left a circle of cold behind it. "I'm so sorry," she said. "You know now it was none of my doing, coming here. Did you think I was dead?"

"*I* didn't. But people said—nasty things. And I think Dad started to believe them."

My mother drew my head to her strangely unyielding breast and held me awkwardly. "My poor boy," she said, jerking me back and forth in a parody of rocking. "My poor sweet boy. But soon it will all be over. We'll all be together again."

I would never have believed my mother's touch could be more creepy than comforting. Had I really come all this way and endured so much, only to find a woman who looked like my mother but felt like a total stranger? Maybe the Great One *was* like one of those cruel and vengeful pagan gods, after all. With a particularly nasty sense of humor.

I pulled myself out of her strained embrace and dashed my sleeve across my eyes. No Flattened Falendan could feel enough to cry. "We don't want to be conspicuous." I gave her a pale smile.

Meli broke into my thoughts. "Ask her what we must do to rescue my parents and the others. We have to free them before tomorrow night."

I translated, but my mother shook her head. "Oh, no, children. That's impossible. The prison is heavily guarded. No one goes in and out but the guards themselves. There's no way we can rescue them."

These words hit my ears like a slap. My mother had never been one to give up so easily. "But—you got out!"

For a split second her eyes went vacant. "A fluke. It could never happen again. Especially now—they will have missed me and doubled the watch."

"We could do like they do in films. You know, knock out a few guards and steal their uniforms."

My mother gave me a pitying smile. "All the guards are at

least six feet tall. You've grown, Danny, but not that much."

My heart sank, not so much because of the difficulties as because of her attitude. "Then we could hide in a laundry cart or something and sneak in that way."

"Goods are unloaded at the gate. Carts aren't allowed to pass through. Believe me, Danny, there's really no way to get in."

Meli's voice was insistent in my mind. I relayed the conversation to her and could feel the desperation in her reply. "But we must rescue them! How can we possibly succeed without them?"

I translated this to my mother. Her face went blank.

"We can't succeed. It's hopeless. I'm sorry, Meli, but we can't save your world. There's nothing for Danny and me to do but return to our own."

I shrank away from this woman who looked like my mother, claimed to be my mother, but spoke words I knew my mother would never say. "No," I said. "I can't give up. Not when I've come so far, gone through so much. And if we fail, this whole world will become like the City. It'll be even worse than ours. I can't let that happen. We have to at least try."

She shook her head. "My own Danny. Always the crusader. I remember the games we used to play—you were always saving me from the villains. But this is the real world, Danny—not *our* world, but still real. You're growing up. You have to accept that sometimes the bad guys win."

I jumped to my feet. "No! I won't accept it! And the mother I remember would never have wanted me to." My eyes bored into hers, but I couldn't get past their glazed surface. "What's happened to you? How can you be saying these things? You never used to be a quitter."

She stretched her hand toward my face again, but I knocked

it away. "Seven years in prison have changed me, Danny. Not on the outside, but on the inside. I know now that evil is strong, stronger than good. We can't stop it. The best we can do is try to protect ourselves."

Her words wrung my heart like a sponge.

I turned to Meli. "I have heard it all in your thoughts, Danny," she thought to me. "But you know we must go on regardless."

"I know. But we can't do anything tonight with that blasted curfew. Let's find our rooms and get some sleep." I couldn't bear this conversation any longer.

"Meli and I are going to get some sleep," I said aloud, "and tomorrow we're going to find a way to rescue her parents and destroy the Dome. If we have to do it without you, we will. I'm sorry, but that's the way it has to be."

My mother rose with a fond, pitying smile that turned my stomach to a block of ice. "I could use some rest myself. We'll talk more in the morning." She left the room.

Meli led the way upstairs and paused before a door. "This is your room. I am next door." She blushed purple.

I started. We'd been traveling together, sleeping near each other, so long it hadn't occurred to me we'd be separated now. But if we were staying in a hotel on Earth, there's no way I'd share a room with a girl who wasn't my sister. I felt my own cheeks redden at the thought.

The hallway was deserted except for us. Meli put her hand in mine. It was soft and warm. "Danny—I am sorry about your mother. I know it must be hard for you to find her so different."

Hard? It was more agonizing than anything I'd had to face in all my far-from-easy life.

"But when we have succeeded," Meli went on, "when we have broken the power of the Dome, perhaps all this evil will be undone and she will be as she was before."

"She'd better be. Or I'll think your Great One cut me a pretty raw deal."

Meli repeated her grandfather's words from when he gave me this crazy assignment—could it be only six days ago? "The Great One's ways are often inscrutable, but always good." She raised her hand to her forehead in a gesture I hadn't seen before. "I will pray to the Great One for her recovery."

I supposed it wouldn't hurt to try a prayer of my own. *Great One, help us. If I can't take her back to Father as she was before, there's not much point in going back at all.*

I WOKE AT FIRST LIGHT, my body aching from fitful sleep, my heart aching with a sadness I now thought I'd never be rid of. I reached for my belt-pouch on the table beside the bed. The Purple Emperor lifted to show the old familiar photo. At least that hadn't changed. The smile in Mum's picture crinkled her whole face, and her eyes sparkled with some delicious joke. I thought of the dead eyes and pitying smile of the mother I'd been reunited with, and my gut twisted.

I dressed and met Meli in the corridor.

"Good morning," she thought to me. "Did you sleep well?"

"Not very. You know."

"I know." She slipped her hand in mine as we went down the stairs. Her hand felt smooth and delicate, and it sent warmth all through me.

In the dining room, I looked for my mother, but she didn't appear. Something in me relaxed.

"We need a plan," I thought to Meli as we ate. "What do you

145

know about this place, this dungeon?"

"Very little. Only what your mother told us, if—forgive me, Danny—if her words are to be trusted."

"We'll have to go see for ourselves, I suppose. Meli—don't you think it's weird she wasn't trying to hide? I mean, if she escaped, they'd be after her. And with her eyes she wouldn't be hard to spot. For that matter, why aren't they after *us*? Surely the nikhi can sense we're here?"

"I think they must, but for some reason they are biding their time. Danny, has it occurred to you—I know this is painful, but—is it possible your mother could be a spy?"

As soon as Meli voiced it, I found the same suspicion lurking at the bottom of my heart. "The mother I knew would never do such a thing. But she's not the mother I knew."

"Perhaps if you pretended to go along with her, that might be our best chance of getting into the Tower." She cut another slice of cheese. "Are you certain she is not able to read your thoughts?"

"Pretty sure. I certainly can't read hers. Her mind is like a wall. Not a solid wall—more like a thick cloud. When I talk with you, I feel your mind probing around inside mine. I don't feel anything like that with her."

"That is good. My guess is that her mind has been taken over—what would be Flattening for us—so she can hear the Enemy's voice, but no other. In that case we may be able to deceive her. It is a thing I abominate, but—what was that you said yesterday? We must be wise as—what?"

"Serpents. They're long skinny reptiles that slither along the ground. I haven't seen anything like that here." I summoned a series of mental pictures for her benefit: a rattlesnake coiled to strike, a cobra with hood spread and fangs bared, a boa constrictor smothering its prey. "They're pretty nasty. And sneaky. We have a—well, a legend, I suppose you'd call it, though it's part of our religion—that all the evil in our world first came from a serpent."

Meli stared. "Your world is very strange, Danny. And yet I wish I could visit it. I would like to see such wonders for myself."

"I wish you could too. There's a lot I'd like to show you."

If I did find my way home—hopefully with my mother restored to her true self—I would have to leave Meli. Something wrenched inside me at the thought.

"Are you finished?" I asked her. "We should go. Do reconnaissance or something." Her eyebrows quirked up in puzzlement. "You know, scope the place out. Case the joint. Get the lay of the land." Her eyes widened even more, and I laughed shortly. "Go to the Tower and see what it's really like. Figure out how to get in."

Her face cleared, and she laughed with me. "Yes. Let us go."

CHAPTER TWENTY-ONE

In Which I Lead a Breakout

WE SET OFF UP THE main street, Meli walking a few paces behind me. From here, in what passed for morning light in the City, I could see the Tower of Grozlukh looming up ahead. Straight and black, it pierced the haze that obscured the Dome and lost its upper stories in the murk.

The stench was overpowering now. I coughed so hard I had to stop walking and double over, wondering if I'd ever breathe freely again. No wonder the City-dwellers couldn't sing—my throat felt like someone had poured acid down it. What if, when the time came for singing, all I could do was croak?

And here, too, the din inside my head got louder, and I could catch a bit of the sense behind the babble: *Work till you drop so you can buy useless things and pursue superficial pleasures to numb the pain of living in this ghastly place.* I wanted to clap my hands to my ears, but it would only make me conspicuous. The faces around me showed no expression as they hurried about their pointless affairs. Clearly the noise no longer bothered them.

I looked back at Meli. If it was bad for me, it must be

unbearable for her. She looked pale and sick, her lavender color already tinged with gray, and she stumbled as she walked. I had to fulfill my mission and get her out of here—fast.

The broad main street ended at the square that held the Tower. I stopped short of the cobbled pavement surrounding it and waited for Meli to catch up. Her breathing was ragged.

The sides of the Tower sloped inward, completely smooth, the glossy black of polished obsidian. Guards stood all around the base. As my mother had warned me, they were tall, armored head-to-toe, with breastplates and visors like black glass. They stood motionless, resting their gauntleted hands on the pommels of immense broadswords—the first weapons I'd seen in Falenda. The Tower had no windows or doors that I could see, but at the center of the side facing us the ranks of guards angled outward. The door must be hidden there.

It looked like my mother was right: it was impossible. The din in my head took on a new undertone: *You have failed, you must fly. You have failed, you must fly.* Maybe the bad guys really were going to win.

Meli's thought-voice broke through. "I hear it too, Danny. But you must resist these thoughts. You must shout them down with truth. Everything that babble says is a lie, for lies are all the Enemy knows. We have not failed until we give up, and we must not give up."

"I don't want to give up. But how can we succeed? How could we ever get in there to rescue your parents, or get to the top from outside? I'm afraid I left my Spiderman gear at home."

Meli ignored that. "Our parents did it seven years ago. Somehow they reached the top."

And now they were inside. I bent my mind to the problem of getting in. The old distraction trick could hardly work on dozens of guards at once. And how could we open that door, with no visible lock or knob? The Doctor would have found a way. Oh, for a bit of psychic paper and a sonic screwdriver!

I heard a commotion coming up the street and spun around. Citizens were scuttling to either side of the wide avenue to make way for a contingent of guards, who were shouting something in the rough City dialect. Meli and I hurried out of the way. As the guards came nearer, between their black helmets I glimpsed several gray turbans.

"Meli! It's the second group of farmers. They've been captured too!"

Her face came alive. "This is our chance! They will open the door now. I think I can get us in. I can become unnoticeable, and if we stay close, I may be able to protect you as well."

"Wow. Is there anything you can't do with those nousíniki of yours?"

"You must not expect too much. I have little practice, and the City has weakened me. The illusion may not be perfect, and it may not last as long as we need. The danger will still be great."

At this point I didn't give a fig for danger, as long as we had a chance of success. I grabbed Meli's hand and pulled her into the street behind the rear guard.

"Do not try to speak to me," she said. "I will need all my concentration. You must take the lead and find our way. And whatever you do, do not let go of my hand."

Nothing seemed to change as Meli performed her magic. But it must have been working, because no one challenged us as we followed close behind the guards, through the yawning black gate and into the Tower of Grozlukh—the Enemy's own stronghold.

The Tower was as black inside as out—walls, floors, ceilings all gleamed like enamel in the greenish light that spilled out of the walls. The air in here was even fouler than outside, and the din in my head pounded like a regiment of oliphaunts. I glanced at Meli. Would she be able to keep her concentration? Her face was drawn, but intent.

On the chance they'd take the new prisoners to where Marala and the others were held, I kept close behind the rear rank of goose-stepping guards. They marched down a long corridor, then turned aside to a stairway. Here each guard grabbed one prisoner by the arm and dragged him down the steps toward the dungeon. Meli and I followed, still unseen.

The stairs went down in a straight line for several stories. At the end the guards pushed the prisoners through a doorway into a corridor. About fifty meters along, they halted at a door where a sentry kept watch. I pulled Meli along the opposite wall and stopped a few paces farther on, where we had a clear view of the door.

One of the incoming guards spoke a few words. The sentry answered, then took off his heavy glove and laid his hand on the door. It slid open. Meli gasped, and I saw Marala's face inside the cell. I knew Marala would sense our presence, so I thought to her, "If you can help us, we might be able to get you out."

"Keep still until all these other guards are gone. Then I will hypnotize the sentry," she answered.

"Right." I pressed myself against the wall as if I could blend into it.

The guards shoved the prisoners into the cell, slid the door shut, and marched off toward the stairs.

Meli's hand trembled in mine. Her face was contorted and

pale. The guard at the door turned in our direction, muttering to himself. He raised his visor and squinted toward us.

"Marala, hurry! Meli's weakening. I think he's seen us!"

The guard growled a curse and started toward us. He groped out with his gauntlet, his fingers millimeters from Meli's nose, and she went stiff with panic. Neither of us breathed. I could have sung a whole cantata in the time we stood there petrified.

Then suddenly the guard's face went slack. His outstretched arms fell to his sides and he crumpled to the floor.

"Quickly, Danny!" came Marala's thought. "I cannot hold him long. Take his hand and place it against the door."

Pulling Meli with me, I stooped beside the unconscious guard and tugged his hand toward the door. The fingertips fell an inch short. I grabbed his legs and dragged him closer. His lips moved and I froze, but he didn't wake up. I ripped off his gauntlet and slammed his palm against the door.

The door slid open. A dozen turbaned Falendans clustered inside it, Marala and Tulamen at the front. Between them they supported a man I hadn't seen before. His skin was pasty gray, stretched taut over his bones, and his nousíniki drooped at half-mast. Meli gave a little gasp when she saw him.

"My husband, Falakúr," Marala thought to me, and in her face was a fierce pride mixed with an aching sorrow. "They have nearly starved him, but still he resists. He can move only slowly now. The rest of you must go on ahead."

"Right. This way." I ran back to the stairs. At the foot of them I strained my ears for the sound of boots. Nothing. "Let's go."

I started up at a lope, Meli beside me, the others close behind. Tulamen lifted Falakúr in his arms and brought up the rear. True Falendans move quietly as a rule, but our breathing and the rustling of our tunics resounded like an army of flapping falcons in the stark stairwell.

"Marala, can you make us inconspicuous? In case we run into any more guards?"

"Not with so many. Even Meli and I together could not, and her strength is spent."

"We'll just have to pray our luck holds out then."

"Not luck, Danny," came Meli's weakened thought-voice. "The Great One's protection."

"Whatever." Maybe *luck* was just another word for the Great One's protection.

I sprinted up the first, underground flights, thinking we'd be safer once we passed the ground floor. But just as I came up to that landing, already gasping for breath, a figure stepped out onto it.

My heart stopped before my feet did. But it wasn't a black-uniformed guard. It was a woman in gray. My mother.

"Well, Danny," she said with that half-mocking smile that froze my blood. "So you've decided to try on your own, despite what I told you. You've become quite independent since I've been gone." She looked past me at the Falendans crowding the stairway and her eyebrows rose. "And you've freed the others after all. I'm impressed. But don't think that means you'll be able to break down the Dome. The guards will be after you any minute."

"Not unless you alert them." I kept my voice low. "How did you get in here?"

"I know a secret way underground. It comes out beyond the square. That's how I escaped yesterday."

I wanted to believe her, but the skin on my arms prickled. The air was thick with danger. "You escaped. So why did you come back?"

She put out a stiff arm. "To be with you, of course. I'm going to climb the Tower with you. But not to help you waste your strength for nothing. Our way home begins from the top of this Tower."

She couldn't mean what I thought she meant. She couldn't be *that* mad.

I started up the next flight at a run, but she caught at my arm with brittle fingers. "Pace yourself. This Tower is hundreds of stories high. It'll take all day to reach the top."

She was right about that. I set off again at a steady pace. My mother climbed beside me. I felt her presence like a chill fog, its tentacles pulling at my courage and resolve. It took so much strength to fight her, when the child inside me just wanted to give up and let her lead me as I had always trusted her to do.

Meli and the others followed close behind. Marala's voice came into my mind. "Danny, I know it is hard for you, but do not trust her. She is not the Celia I once knew. I fear she is working for the Enemy."

"I know she is. But we still have to get to the top. Maybe the guards will leave us alone while she's with us."

Marala fell silent, and we climbed on.

CHAPTER TWENTY-TWO

In Which I Sing for My Mother

W E CLIMBED SO LONG I forgot everything except drag-
ging one foot up after the other. Every so often the stair
would make a right-angle turn, following the outside walls. At
each landing we paused to get our breath, but the foulness of
the air seared our lungs. On top of that, the din in my mind
was so loud I felt like I was sitting in the front row at a heavy
metal concert. My stomach was the abyss of Moria. My throat
was the Sahara in a dry year.

Meli and the others were struggling as much as I was.
"Aren't your nousíniki giving you a boost?" I thought to her at
the fourth or fifth rest.

"No. Their power is waning under this onslaught. I need all
their strength just to fight off the noise."

At each break, Falakúr was passed from one man to another,
hanging limp in their arms. My mother seemed tireless. She
leaned against the wall, breathing easily, until we were ready
to go on. Perhaps her exercise during her years in prison had
consisted of climbing these stairs.

Each flight was a little shorter than the last, as the sides of the Tower sloped gradually inward. When I figured we were about halfway up, I realized some of the pounding in my head was coming in through my ears. I paused and tried to focus them downward. I heard a distant thumping sound, like a centipede in boots tromping up the stone stairs.

"They're after us!" I said aloud. "We've got to move faster."

My mother smiled slightly and kept her maddeningly even pace. I pushed past her at a run, but within half a flight I had to slow down again. We were still too far from the top to sprint. And meanwhile the tromping got louder.

We plodded on until the flights dwindled to a dozen steps apiece. We had to be getting close. "Come on!" I thought to the others, and dug into my reserves for one last push. The stairs ended at a door—a smooth door like the ones in the dungeon, with no knob, no handle, no keyhole. I put my palm against it, but it didn't budge.

My mother came up behind me. "Why such a hurry, son? The guards won't stop us from going home." I made way for her, and she laid her palm against the black surface. The door slid back. If I needed any further proof she was working for the Enemy, I had it now. The door was programmed to her touch.

We poured through onto a flat rooftop about ten feet square, with a low, solid parapet on all sides. Above us was thick darkness, like a cloudy night, with two faint spots glowing through it a few inches apart. "The Moons," Meli thought to me. "The smaller is Anílena and the larger is Núlatel. In a few minutes they will merge."

"Good. Those guards can't be far behind now." I glanced back at the door as it slid shut behind the last of the Falendans. We couldn't lock the door, and there was nothing to use for a barricade. "Tulamen, you and the others stand to each side. Try to stop the guards as they come through."

Tulamen nodded, and he and the other men ranged themselves against the wall. They had no weapons, though. What could they do against broadswords?

My mother crossed to the far parapet and beckoned to me. "Come, Danny. This is our way home."

I stared at her. She really meant it. She *was* mad.

"You don't seriously want us to fall from this Tower."

"That is the only way to travel between worlds."

"But—the elúndina can't get through the Dome. How could they carry us to our world if we fell from here?"

Her mouth twisted. "What makes you think elúndina are necessary? Other beings have the same power."

I fell back as if an invisible hand had pushed me hard in the chest. "The nikhi?" I whispered. "You'd trust yourself to the *nikhi?*"

"Why not? The Dark One wants us out of his world. Why shouldn't he send his servants to take us away?"

I clutched my head. It felt as if two armies were battling inside it. The din of the Dome was now focused into one shout, so loud in my mind I couldn't hear my own thoughts. *Trust her,* it hammered. *Go with her. She is your mother. Didn't you come here to find her? Go with her home to your father. You will be a happy family again.*

The din faded, and my mind filled with a picture of myself and my mother—her true self again—being returned gently to Earth and running to meet my father, the three of us locked in a rapturous embrace, dancing and singing in the street—

Singing. That was what I had come here to do. Like the clear, high voice of a flute rang the unconquerable truth of what Meli had told me: The Enemy *always* lies. No way could a moment of cowardice lead to happiness.

The booted footsteps pounded louder, much too close below us. The moons were almost touching. The Falendans stood taut and ready; their keyed-up impatience shimmered at the edges of my mind. I should be singing now.

I faced my mother. "No. That is not the way. Fight the lie, Mother! The Enemy doesn't want us gone. He wants us *dead*. He wants our bodies crushed to powder at the bottom of this Tower."

Her eyes flickered for a moment, then dulled. "My poor deluded boy. It's impossible, what you're trying to do. What, this poor company you've collected sing down the mightiest Dome ever built? It's laughable. And if you did succeed, what then? The whole City would crumble to dust—including this Tower we're standing on. And the Dark One's servants wouldn't save you then. It's suicide, Danny." Her iron fingers clamped onto my arm even as her voice softened to the sweet crooning I remembered from bedtimes long ago. "Don't deprive me of my son forever now that I've finally got you back. Come, my darling. Come back to real life."

I wavered. She must be telling the truth about one thing: if we succeeded, we would die. My body would lie buried forever under piles of rubble in a foreign world, and my father would never know what had become of me.

"It's not fair," I whispered. "I'm only thirteen years old. I shouldn't have to make this kind of choice."

I looked up. The smaller of the two glowing moons snuggled up against the rim of the larger like a child leaning into its mother's embrace. Their light grew brighter, dispelling the haze, until the two globes were sharply outlined against the

black sky. A faint throbbing hum emitted from them, growing louder. In seconds they would fully converge.

The pounding of booted feet grew to a crescendo of kettle-drums behind the door.

"The guards, Danny!" It was Meli's voice, so dear to me, now that I was sure of losing her. "Hurry! Sing!"

I looked at my mother, her eyes lifeless in a mask of angry

command. Behind me the Falendans all stood together, their faces full of fierce determination, calling out to me with one wordless voice—the voice of love.

"Sing, Danny!" Marala's thought-voice said. "Sing for the defeat of the Evil that has possessed your mother. Sing for the salvation of Falenda. Sing for the triumph of the good!"

I turned toward my mother and began the song that had been playing in my mind all day:

O Danny boy, the pipes, the pipes are calling
From glen to glen and on the mountainside
The summer's gone, and all the roses dying
It's you, it's you must go and I must bide.

Her face went livid. For a moment her eyes returned to life, wide and horrible. Her hand unclamped from my arm and she jerked backward toward the parapet like a marionette.

I watched, struck stiff with horror but still singing, until her back struck the wall. Then I forced my feet to life, ran to her, and grabbed for her outstretched hands. Our fingertips touched, and hers were warm and yielding again. My heart ripped in half.

Then through the murk I saw the nikhi swarming around her. They beat my hands away and yanked her up onto the parapet. She swayed there for the space of an anguished heartbeat, then toppled into the void.

CHAPTER TWENTY-THREE

In Which Is the End of All Things

M Y SONG DIED IN MY throat. I threw myself at the parapet and stretched one arm down, almost out of its socket. But my mother was already far below, her inert body sliding down the slick slope of the Tower. "Mother!" I cried with all that was in me, but my cry only echoed back to me, mockingly, out of the void.

The guards burst through the door behind me, shouting in the rough City dialect.

"Danny, don't stop! Keep singing!" came Meli's voice. "You can't save her now, but you can still save us!"

I straightened and struggled to force down the thing in my throat that threatened to strangle me. But just as I took a breath to sing, black gauntlets pinioned my arms behind me and pulled me back against a cold, hard breastplate.

I turned my head to see the Falendans fighting like berserkers, using some sort of Falendan jujitsu. Falakúr disarmed one guard with a kick to the wrist. Lodamor ducked as another came at him, and before I could blink, the guard was sprawled on the roof. Even Ruávena twisted out of her guard's grasp and kicked his feet out from under him.

But guards kept pouring through the door like nikhi out of the forest, four or five of them to each of us. Sheer numbers prevailed, and soon my friends were overpowered and pinned just as I was.

My guard dragged me toward the door. *It's over,* I thought. *I've failed.*

"No, Danny! It is not over. Sing! We will help you, but you must begin. Now, Danny! Sing!"

I looked up into Meli's anguished face. She still believed in me. The last spark of my courage flickered into life.

Mentally I raced through my repertoire, searching for the perfect song to banish the darkness from this sleeping City once and for all. Then I filled my lungs and let soar the hymn that had always been my favorite:

My life goes on in endless song
Above earth's lamentations,
I hear the real, though far-off hymn
That hails a new creation.

The others joined the song with their own harmonies, and my quavering voice steadied and grew.

When tyrants tremble, sick with fear,
And hear their death-knell ringing,
When friends rejoice both far and near,
How can I keep from singing?

Now, to my amazement, I heard myself taking off from the original rhythms, improvising a melody that exactly fitted the task I had been sent to do.

In prison cell and dungeon vile,
Our thoughts to them go winging;
When friends by shame are undefiled,
How can I keep from singing?

The music swelled outward from the Tower and filled the night.

No storm can shake my inmost calm,
While to that rock I'm clinging.
Since love is lord of heaven and earth
How can I keep from singing?

The guard that held me slowed. He had me almost at the door when I heard a moan behind me, then my arms were suddenly free. I turned and saw the guard crouching, writhing, his hands clapped over his ears. The other guards fell one by one. Our music had the same effect on their Flattened minds as the Enemy's Noise did on the True Falendans.

I held out my hands to my friends, and they moved to form a circle around me. The glowing moons overlapped and merged into one white sphere as brilliant as the sun. I reached into my gut and poured all my love for my mother and father, all the joys and sufferings of my life at home, all the strength and wisdom I'd gained in Falenda, and all my affection for my new Falendan family into my song. I knew the others were doing the same. We were only a dozen voices, but our song broke through the haze and rang out against the gemlike facets of the Dome.

The air trembled above me as the final chorus rose to its crescendo. The moons' hum now answered the singing like a string orchestra playing fortissimo. I emptied my lungs into a high C and held it. Then I heard a crash of splintering crystal that multiplied into a mighty roar. The floor shook beneath my feet.

Bracing our feet and clinging to each other, we sang the cadenza. Huge fragments of multicolored crystals rained down around us. A cold and mighty wind rushed in, driving off the last tentacles of haze and filling our lungs with blessed clean air. The two moons bathed the rooftop in a molten diamond light.

This is it, I thought. *This is the end.* I squeezed Meli's hand.

The Tower gave a convulsive heave, throwing us into each other's arms. Across the City all the buildings were swaying, cracking, crumbling, as jagged chasms tore through the streets.

A great screaming wail came up from the ground. A monstrous shadow rose before us, blotting out the moons. It hovered over us, screeching like the feedback from a hundred amplifiers, until I thought my ears would burst. We crouched, cowering under its blast of sheer hatred. Then, with a final wail, it shriveled in on itself and was gone.

The Tower swayed like a pendulum, a little farther each time. *We're done for now,* I thought. *But it was worth it.* Meli's eyes shone so that I thought my heart would burst.

I clutched her as the swaying threw us down to the rooftop and we slid from parapet to parapet. "Meli—" I began, but broke off. The air was full of bits of color, which I had taken for fragments of the collapsing Dome. But now I realized the bits weren't falling, they were flying—toward us.

"Meli! It's the elúndina!"

We scrambled to our feet as hundreds of the Great One's servants surrounded our group. Just as the Tower gave one last mighty lurch, the elúndina lifted us on their brilliant wings. I watched the Tower crumble underneath where my feet had been a moment before.

"My mother!" I cried to the elúndina with a last wild hope. "Can you save my mother?"

They didn't answer, but a flock of them broke off and swooped down toward the shrieking chaos below.

Underneath us the rumbling, heaving mass sent up thick clouds of dust. I turned away, my throat burning. All those people . . . I hoped against hope for my mother's salvation, but I knew all the rest of the City's population must be lost.

"I know, Danny," came Meli's thought-voice. "They are my people, and their death rips the flesh from my bones. But they were all Flattened beyond helping. All that was good and true in them died years ago. It is only empty husks that are being crushed now."

Even so, those husks deserved a funeral. I started in low on the *Kyrie* from Mozart's *Requiem*, and the others joined me in lamentation. We hovered over the chaos like a choir of angels, baptizing the ruins with our tears. *Kyrie eleison. Lord, have mercy on this Flattened race.*

CHAPTER TWENTY-FOUR

In Which There Is Great Rejoicing

THE ELÚNDINA CARRIED US UP into the clear night sky, where the two moons had now crossed and were pulling apart, reaching arms of light toward each other as if the child-moon were being ripped from its mother's embrace. Where was my mother? Had the elúndina gotten to her in time? I couldn't see a sign of them below. The Tower was hundreds of stories high, but the song had taken some time. If only I'd paid attention in science class, I might have remembered something about terminal velocity. As it was, I would just have to wait.

I expected to be put down just out of harm's way, but the elúndina flew on as far as Tulamen's village. There we all touched down, and the whole village came out to meet us. They sang and danced in the crisp night air—the stench of Haka-grug was quickly fading. I was distracted for a while as we sang farewell to the nine villagers who had helped us, and the girls of the village crowned me with a wreath of tílamel vines.

Tulamen and the others offered us lodging for the night—Marala, Falakúr, Meli, and me—but we were anxious to get back to Kalotelaméliku, Meli's home village, and give them the good news. The elúndina bore us up again and carried us onward—down the cliffs, past Marala's cave, and across the endless plain, now a silvery grey in the moonlight.

It was a strange flight, but not an uncomfortable one. We must have been traveling faster than a commercial jet, yet I didn't feel the speed and had no fear of falling. But as soon as I was alone with my thoughts again, all I could think about was my mother. I looked back again and again, but couldn't see anyone following us. What if they'd been too late? What if she lay crushed and buried within those tragic ruins? I had saved Falenda—but at what unbearable cost?

When at last we were all set down at the entrance to the cavern of Kalotelaméliku, I got up the courage to ask the elúndina who carried me whether my mother had been rescued. "Our brothers are following," was all they would answer. "They will soon be here."

By this time the moons had set, and the forest hid the sky beyond the small clearing. I could see nothing, do nothing but wait. It took all the strength I had left to keep myself from shattering into pieces from the strain.

"Thank you," I said to the elúndina. "Thank you for saving our lives."

A rustling of wings. "Do not thank us. We only serve the will of the Great One. Thank him."

"Come, Danny," Meli thought to me. "Let us go inside. They will be waiting."

With a last glance at the empty sky, I followed Meli and her parents into the tunnel.

When we came out into the open square of the village, I squinted at the sudden light. Hundreds of heads of glowing nousíniki lit the farthest reaches of the cavern. All the villagers, from tots to ancient geezers, bustled about the square, getting ready for a feast that made our dinner in the tree-village look like a light snack. Low tables filled with every imaginable kind of fruit, dozens of different cheeses, mounds of mouth-watering pastries, and elaborate dishes I couldn't begin to identify. My stomach growled like a whole pride of lions. I hadn't eaten since breakfast the morning before, and now a new day was about to dawn.

Meli got my attention. "I must go with my mother and help my father to bed. He is not strong enough to partake of this feast."

The emaciated Falakúr leaned heavily on the shoulders of his wife and daughter. "Will he recover?"

Marala answered, "Now that the power of the Enemy is broken, yes, he will recover—given time, careful nursing, and a great deal of rest. I will take him to our old chamber and rejoin you in time for the feast."

"In the meantime—" Meli looked me up and down with a mischievous grin. "You may wish to bathe."

I glanced at my arms, still gray with garáma juice, and laughed. "I might, at that."

A small boy showed me to a room with a calivóda bath and handed me a sponge and a small pot of yellow goo. "This will remove the garama stain," he said.

I slathered on the goo, then sank into the calivoda and watched the gray color dissolve. When my skin was a healthy pink again, I dozed, then awoke to find a clean tunic and rope sandals ready for me.

I found the old logosagami, Meli's grandfather, just outside. "Danny," he said, "someone is waiting for you. Come, let us go to her." He beckoned to a young man to follow and led the way out into the clearing.

There, amid the violet grasses at the tunnel's mouth, a crumpled figure lay, elúndina fluttering around it. A gray hood had fallen back to reveal blonde hair wrapped in braids around her head.

"Mother!" The elúndina made way for me at her side. She was so still, so pale, so cold. "Is she alive?"

"She lives," the logosagami answered. "The elúndina can travel in time as well as in space, and thus were able to catch her before she touched the ground. But her body has come close to death, and her soul even closer. She will need all my skill to heal her. You must remain with us yet a while, Danny, until she is strong enough to return home."

"Then—we will be going home? Eventually?"

"Oh, yes. The Great One has work for you in your own world."

"Work? What kind of work? There aren't any domes to sing down in my world."

"Perhaps not. But you have an Enemy of your own there whose influence is great. We will talk of this another time. Now is the time to feast and give thanks to the Great One for your victory."

The young man lifted my mother gently in his arms, and we all returned through the tunnel. I wanted to follow where they were taking her, but the logosagami laid a hand on my arm. "She will be well cared for. There is nothing you can do for her at this time. Come and join the feast. You are the guest of honor."

He led me to the top table, where Meli and Marala were waiting. They had changed into long gowns and removed their blue eye-shields. Meli's eyes shone with a golden light that warmed my heart as I took my place next to her. Behind the shelter of her gown she slipped her hand into mine.

The logosagami raised his hands, and the last servers scuttled to their places in silence. "My people," he said, "we gather this day to give thanks to the Great One for our deliverance from the great evil that has threatened our land. The power of the Dome has been broken. Once again, all Falenda will live in harmony.

"We gather also to honor our Deliverer, Danny, and his companions, who struggled bravely in the face of great peril. And we rejoice to welcome my daughter, Marala, and her husband, Falakúr, who have returned to us at last."

At this a deafening cheer broke out. People stomped, clinked their glasses, drummed on the tables, and shouted for all they were worth. I'd never imagined True Falendans could get so rowdy. My mouth stretched into a silly grin.

The logosagami raised his hands again, and the noise subsided. "Now we will sing our thanksgiving to the Great One." He turned to me. "Deliverer, will you lead us in song?"

I launched into "Praise God, from whom all blessings flow." One by one the Falendans joined in with their harmony and counterpoint, and the song swelled until the cavern's crystal roof rang with joyous praise.

I realized in that moment I did not want to go home. I wanted to stay with these simple, joyful, loving people forever. And—with Meli. Beneath my song I added a private prayer: *Please, if I have to go home, let me come back someday and see Meli again.*

She squeezed my hand, and I knew she was thinking the same.

AFTER THE FEAST WAS OVER, I slept around the clock. The next morning, I asked if I could see my mother.

"You may see her," the logosagami answered, "but do not expect a great improvement as yet."

He led me to a room where my mother lay on a raised pallet. A Falendan woman was sponging her arms with calivóda. When I came in, the woman got up and made way for me to sit on the bed.

My mother was still very pale, though not quite as white as before. When I touched her cheek, it was warm under my hand. But she lay unmoving, eyes closed; I could hardly tell she was breathing.

"Mum," I whispered. "It's me, Danny. Come back to me, Mum. I came here to rescue you. You have to come back."

I held her hand between my own and bent down to kiss her forehead. Her eyelids fluttered slightly, then she was still. If she didn't wake up, if her mind could not be restored, what good did it do to have her body whole? I couldn't take the empty husk of her back to my father.

"Her body is mending," the logosagami said, "but its healing can progress only so far without the healing of her soul. I must tend to her now. It will be best if you go. You may come again in the evening. Go and enjoy yourself with Meli." He smiled.

Reluctantly, I went. I met Meli in the corridor. Falakúr's sickroom was next door.

"How is your father?"

She looked somber. "He is still very weak. He wakes only to take nourishment, then sleeps again. But he will be well in time. And your mother?"

"Not much improvement yet. But your grandfather seems

to think he can heal her eventually." I studied the toe of my sandal. "He said you and I should enjoy ourselves."

Her face lit. "What about a balikuni ride?"

"All right."

We went out into the clearing. The stable was off to one side. As soon as we turned in that direction, I heard a loud honking, and two balikuni came charging toward us. The larger one stopped in front of me and nuzzled me with its horn.

"Vali!" I cried and threw my arms around his neck. The honking subsided to a purr. I pulled back to scratch at the base of his horn. "How did you get here so fast? We left you at Marala's, clear across the plains."

I looked into Vali's eyes and saw a mental picture of the two balikuni galloping across the violet meadow. Meli had more practice in communicating with animals. She listened to Nila for a minute, then explained. "When the Dome shattered, the earthquake shook the ground as far as my mother's clearing. The animals knew what had happened and that we would be carried here, so they galloped all the way home. Their endurance is amazing, and they can make quite good time without riders to weigh them down."

I stroked Vali's neck. "But you must be tired and hungry. You won't be up for a ride just yet."

Vali tossed his head and honked. I saw a mental picture of the two balikuni enjoying a big feed and a good rest. Vali turned his left side toward me and nudged me with his horn.

"Well, if you insist—let's ride!"

I vaulted neatly onto Vali's back. Meli mounted Nila, and we set off along a forest path.

It was early in the morning, and the shadows were deep under the orange malacána trees. I still felt a little nervous about shadows. "What about the nikhi? Are they all gone?"

Meli nodded. "They existed only by Hakagrug's power, and his power is broken forever. The nikhi will not trouble us again."

I raised my voice in a great shout that turned into song— this time, "Morning Has Broken." It was good to be alive in a nikhi-free world.

CHAPTER TWENTY-FIVE

In Which I Say Hello and Goodbye

WHEN WE GOT BACK TO the cavern, I looked in on my mother. The logosagami was bending over her, holding a cloth to her forehead as she thrashed about on the bed.

"What is it? What's happening to her?" I rushed to the bedside.

"She is fevered. But there is no infection. I believe she is reliving all her time in Falenda—especially her time in the City. It must have been terrible."

I groaned. "She said they treated her well, but they did sort of brainwash her. How good can that be?"

I sat on the bed and tried to take her hand, but her arms kept flailing. I had to duck back to avoid being hit in the face. "How long has she been like this? Will she get better?"

"Since midday. I hope she will improve, but this is a case unlike any I have seen before. I can make no promises."

I sprang to my feet and paced the small space, biting my knuckle. "The golden lenafálina! That's good for mind sickness, right? Have you tried that?"

Logosagami looked at me with great patience. "Yes, Danny. That and every other art I know. I think now we can only wait, and stay with her. Time will be our friend."

I lost count of the days I kept watch in my mother's room, leaving only for meals and a few occasional hours of fitful sleep. She was not always restless; sometimes she sank into a stupor so deep I had to hold my hand to her face to make sure she was still breathing.

In her restless times she muttered phrases I could barely make out. I heard my own name, and sometimes my father's, Michael. One word she shouted clearly, again and again: "NO!" That was proof enough for me she'd put up quite a fight against Hakagrug's control of her mind.

During her quiet times, I talked to her about anything that came into my head—life in her absence, the old days when we'd all been together. I sang to her, our old favorite songs and the new ones I'd learned in choir school. I talked and sang until I was hoarse, but it didn't make any difference. She seemed deaf to my voice.

At last, one day, her cool hand lay quietly in mine and her breathing was deep and sure. But she still didn't wake up. The logosagami came in, and I turned to him, half hoping, half dreading what he might say.

"She seems better—is she better? Why doesn't she wake up?"

The logosagami checked her pulse, felt her breathing, raised her closed eyelids, then sat back. "Her body is healed; the fever has left her, I believe for good. But her mind is far from us still."

He probed into my eyes. "It must be you, whom she loves, to call her back. Talk to her of the things she knows. Sing to her."

"I've been doing that all this time. There's nothing left to say, no more songs. I've tried them all." I heard the note of panic in my own voice, and it scared me.

The logosagami looked into me even deeper. "Come with me, Danny. We must talk."

I dragged myself after him into the main room. He made me sit down, though I was too jittery to sit still.

"Danny, you must prepare yourself for the possibility that your mother will not recover."

I jumped up. "What? But you said—you promised—" I stopped myself. He'd been encouraging, but he'd never actually promised me anything.

I paced in front of him. "I can't go back without her healed. I can't face my dad like that. I can't face anything if I don't have her."

The logosagami just looked at me, that old, patient look that made me feel two years old. "Sit down, Danny."

I paced one more circuit, then gave up and dropped onto a cushion.

"What is it that you cannot face?"

I buried my head in my hands and mumbled through my fingers. "Bull. Leaving choir school. Dad's drinking. All of it."

"And why do you think you cannot face these things?"

The words came out of me without thought. "Because I'm no good. I'm an idiot, a coward, a weakling. All I can do is sing."

"Was it a small thing to sing down the Dome?"

"Well, no, but—"

"Was it an idiot who saved Meli when she broke her leg? Was it a coward who defeated Hakagrug? Is it a weakling who has earned my granddaughter's love?"

I raised my head and stared at him as if he were talking about someone else. Meli's love? Me?

"And all of this you did without your mother's help—even against her opposition."

He waited a minute to let that sink in.

"You have the strength within you to live your own life."

His words churned inside me. I tried to fight them down, but they kept springing up again. At last I had to admit they were true. I loved my mother, missed her, wanted her—but if I had to, I could go on living without her. Even on Earth.

The logosagami sensed my acceptance and spoke again. "And I think, if you can only believe it, you may have the strength to call your mother back after all."

I was on my feet in an instant. "How? Haven't we tried everything?"

"I think there is one thing you have not tried. Is there not some object that was precious to you both? Did you not bring it here to Falenda?"

The music box! I dashed to my room, where I'd left my belt pouch. With shaking fingers I fumbled in it until I found the Purple Emperor. I closed it in my fist with a prayer, then ran back.

I pushed aside the curtain to my mother's room and stopped. The music box was my last hope. What if it didn't work? As long as I put off trying it, I could still cling to that hope.

The logosagami beckoned to me, and I forced myself the few steps to her bedside. I knelt and laid the tiny box on her palm.

"Mum," I said. "I brought you our music box—remember? The one Dad gave you. With the picture of the three of us and the plait of our hair? I kept it with me all the time you were gone. Listen."

I pressed the catch and eased the lid open. I could almost

see the tinkling notes making their way from the rotating cylinder to my mother's ear. The box ran through the first verse and half the second, then I joined in, my voice barely above a whisper:

And I shall hear, though soft you tread above me
And all my grave shall warmer, sweeter be
And then ye'll bend and tell me that you love me
And I shall sleep in peace until you come to me.

The box wound down into silence. I leaned over and said in her ear, "I love you, Mum." Then I watched her intently, as if I could see through her skin and bones to her beating heart, as if I could will her into consciousness.

Her eyelids fluttered. I held my breath. I'd never been so still.

She drew in a sharp breath, then exhaled on a sigh. Her eyes opened.

"Mum?" I whispered.

Her eyes swiveled in my direction. "Danny," she said, and smiled.

MUM GOT HER STRENGTH BACK slowly under the logosagami's care. After a week or so, she could sit up a good part of the day. I sat with her, and Meli and Marala came in often; Falakúr was getting strong enough now they could leave him when he slept.

Mum still seemed far away from me. She'd sit quietly, listening to Meli and me talking or singing together; but she hardly ever spoke. She seemed happiest when Marala was around.

That hurt me until Marala explained, in thought-speech intended for only me to hear. "She and I were last together when she was still brave and strong. I saw her at her best; you saw her at her worst. She is ashamed of having yielded to the Enemy's power."

I took my mother's hands. "Mum," I said, "don't feel bad about what happened—I mean, on the Tower. You couldn't help it, I know that."

The shadows under her eyes broke my heart. "I betrayed you," she said. "I betrayed you all—and almost killed my only son."

"But it wasn't really you, Mum. I knew that all along. It was the Enemy using you."

"But I must have let him use me. I didn't fight hard enough. Look at Falakúr—he didn't give in."

Marala shook her head. "You must not compare yourself to Falakúr. You are human, he is Falendan; and the Enemy did not target him in the same way. For him it was only maltreatment and the same assault upon the mind that every Citizen had to endure. For you it was much more intentional. The Enemy knew he would need you to foil the next attempt on the Dome. You must not reproach yourself, Celia. All is well now, and all is forgiven. Only rejoice that your son held firm so that you could be reunited."

Mum's eyes still looked haunted. Marala said to me, "I think she is strong enough now to go outside. Why don't you take her out into the square and show her around?"

I knew what Marala had in mind. "Come on, Mum, let's go out and I'll show you the village. You've been cooped up in here too long."

She sighed, but let me lead her out into the square.

The scene there reminded me of my first morning in Falenda. Everywhere men and women went about their daily tasks, and as they worked they sang their ever-changing song of praise.

Mum stopped on the steps with a hand to her throat. "Oh!" she gasped. "How lovely! I'd forgotten how beautifully they sing."

"Why don't you join in? It's easy. Just sing whatever you want."

"Oh, no, I couldn't. I haven't sung for so long, I'd only croak. You go ahead."

I lifted my voice to join the others. By now I had the knack of it and improvised along with them, letting the music flow from my heart with no interference from my brain. After a while I heard a tentative sound beside me. Mum's voice was a little croaky at first, but as she sang it got stronger, and the general song shaped itself around hers. At last she let go and sang full out, and the song rang up to the crystal ceiling.

When her voice gave out, she fell silent, but the radiance of her face told me Marala's plan had succeeded. Now, with time, the ache in my mother's soul would be able to heal.

Later that day, when we'd toured the village and were resting again in her room, she said to me, "And now, love, it's time for you to tell me what's been happening at home. You haven't said a word about your dad, so I know it can't be good. But I'm strong enough to think about going home. I need to hear what you've been holding back."

I took a deep breath. "Well, you see—when you disappeared, people started to talk. They said horrid things, cruel things. At first Dad wouldn't listen, but when you didn't come back and the police couldn't find you—well, I think he started to believe the rumors. He got—so sad . . ." Here I stopped. I couldn't trust my voice.

"Oh, my poor darlings . . ." Mum pulled me close for a minute, then stood. "We have to get home. Now he thinks he's lost you as well. There's no telling what might happen."

She started to leave the room, but I held her back. "The logosagami says we can go back to any time since the minute I left. Dad might not even know I've been gone. We need to wait till you're strong enough."

She turned back to me and her posture relaxed. "Truly? In that case, it can wait until morning. But no longer. I'm well enough, and I want to be home."

AT DINNER I SAT BY MYSELF, slumped over my plate, picking at the peel of a magenta fruit I had no intention of eating. Meli sat down beside me, her nousíniki agitating about her face. "Is it true? You are leaving tomorrow?"

"My mum wants to go home. She's worried about my dad. Your grandfather says it's time."

Meli put a shy hand on mine. "But you—you do not wish to go?"

I looked at her, my throat burning. "Me? What does it matter what I want?"

"It matters to me."

I turned away, gritting my teeth. "I want . . . I want to be both places at once. Or no—I want to bring my dad here. The rest of it—"

My mind filled with pictures of home. The drab, dirty flat, the everlasting winter drizzle, Bull and his cronies waiting to ambush me. But I also saw the warm stones of the cathedral soaring into the heavens; the surprise of Canon Howard's kind eyes under his threatening brows; the familiar green of trees and grass, the riotous wildflowers of the brief English spring.

"Well, there are a few other things I miss. But not as much as I'll miss—you."

I turned my hand to lace my fingers with hers, then summoned the courage to look into her eyes. I was only going-on-fourteen, and she was a different species. Why should I feel as if my heart were being torn in two?

"I will miss you too, Danny. More than you know. But I think that once two people have known each other as we have done, they have a bond that can never be broken. I cannot say with certainty, for it has never been tried, but I believe that bond will stretch even across the distance between our worlds." She smiled. "And perhaps someday you will return to our world—or perhaps I may be allowed to come to yours."

Hope soared in my heart at these words. "Yes. Someday."

CHAPTER TWENTY-SIX

In Which I Take Bull by the Horns

THE NEXT MORNING, I FOUND my own grey flannel school shorts and jacket lying ready for me, clean and pressed, on a stool, my own brogues and knee socks underneath. With the sight of them, a sudden sharp longing came over me for every tiny detail of my old life: everything from the steamy crunch of hot fish and chips to the thrill of opening a new piece of choir music to the good old everlasting English rain. Without that attack of homesickness, I don't think I would have been able to face what lay before me that day.

I met Mum in the hall. She was dressed in the tweed skirt and pullover she'd been wearing when she disappeared. "Look at us," she said. "These clothes feel so strange now. And I feel so different. I hope your father will recognize me."

"Don't be silly, Mum. He'd know you no matter what. No matter when."

She took my hand, and we went out onto the steps. The villagers were gathered in the square, and as soon as we came out they all began a song of farewell—a song so full of both joy and sorrow that Mum's eyes filled with tears, and I had to bite my lip till it bled. "What wonderful people!" Mum said. "I wish we could take them all home with us." She shot a sidelong glance at me. "Especially Meli, eh?"

I looked down, my face flaming. What would life back at home be like with a mother who could read my thoughts?

The logosagami, Marala, Meli, and Falakúr—who was much stronger and looked almost like a True Falendan again—walked with us through the forest to the open plain. Mum exclaimed over the beauty of the place with every step.

"I'd forgotten how lovely all this was. Oh, Danny, if only we could bring your father here, I think I could stay forever."

I shot a hopeful look at the logosagami, but he shook his head. "I am sorry, but the will of the Great One is for you to return to your own world. But the gate has been opened, and I do not believe it will be closed again for some time. Meanwhile, we will always remember you, and you will remember us."

I said goodbye to each of the adults with the traditional Falendan gesture of placing palm to palm. But when I got to Meli, my palm slipped from hers and I threw my arms around her. "This is how we say goodbye in my world." I finished off with a quick kiss.

When I released her, Meli's cheeks were deep purple and she wouldn't meet my eyes. But she thought to me, "I think I like your way."

I stepped back to Mum's side and drew a deep breath, trying to concentrate on how Dad's face would look when he saw us again.

The logosagami probed my mind. "I believe it will be best if you do not return to exactly the moment you left. We will give your father enough time to miss you. But not enough time to despair."

I did a quick mental calculation. I'd fallen from the bell tower on the twentieth of December, so it must be well past Christmas now. I'd missed my solos in the Service of Lessons and Carols.

"Logosagami, could you get us back for Christmas Eve?"

"I will ask the elúndina. It is for them to decide."

He raised his arms wide, face to the heavens. Within moments, the air was filled with the darting, changing bits of light that were the elúndina.

"Are you ready?" the logosagami asked.

I nodded and gripped Mum's hand. I had just time for a last glance at Meli's shining eyes before we began to rise toward the golden sky, and then everything went black.

WHEN I OPENED MY EYES, I had to sit up and blink a few times before I could focus. I felt cold stone under me, and before me stood the crenellated parapet of the cathedral bell tower. For one horrible second I thought it might all have been a dream. But then I saw my mother beside me, holding her head and looking dazed.

"Mum, we're here! We're home!"

She looked around, blinking. "Where?"

I helped her to her feet so she could see past the parapet. "On the bell tower, Mum. And look—the sun's about to set. Our own yellow sun in a blue sky! Well, partly blue anyway." That was the best you could expect in December. "That means they'll be ringing for Evensong soon. We'd better get down if we don't want to go deaf."

Her face lit with an expression I remembered well. "Race

you down!"

This was an old joke between us, for the narrow stairway couldn't fit two abreast; the first to reach the stairhead was guaranteed to be the winner. I made a convincing dash but let her win.

At the bottom we paused for breath. I followed Mum's gaze across the cobblestoned yard to the ivied brick of the bishop's residence, the smaller houses of the archdeacon, dean, and canons, the solid block of the choir school, the ancient elms that towered over all.

"Everything looks just the same," she said, a mixture of wonder and satisfaction in her tone. "Are you sure it's been seven years?"

I hesitated. How could I be certain the elúndina had really brought us back to the right time? But then I heard the bellowing of Bull and his herd from the alley beyond the school. "Oh yes, Mum. I'm sure."

I set off across the close. I'd gone about fifty meters when the gang burst out of the alleyway. "Well, well, well, look who's here!" Bull jeered. "If it isn't our little truant star soprano! Ooh, he ain't half in trouble, eh, boys? Canon Howard's going to string you up, if your dad doesn't do it first." He stopped and turned to his gang. "Awful hard work for old men, eh, lads? What say we save 'em the trouble?"

I kept walking until the gang had surrounded me. Only then did I realize Mum wasn't at my side. I looked back—she'd stopped to read a notice board by the cathedral door. I planted my feet and faced Bull.

"Where've you been, then, Danny?" Bull said. "Give us a good enough lie and maybe we'll let you off." He turned to his toadies for a laugh, which they obediently supplied.

I looked at Bull's leering face and felt nothing but pity. "Haven't you anything better to do than harass people?" I asked him. "It's none of your business where I've been, but since I'm feeling magnanimous today, I'll tell you: I've been to fetch my mother home."

Bull's mouth dropped open. His eyes moved up to the left, and I sensed my mother coming up beside me. Bull shook himself and pulled up his jaw. "That's never your mum," he sneered. "She's gone and she's not coming back. Must be your auntie, come to look after you like the baby you are."

"You're quite wrong, you know," Mum said. "I am his mother. I was taken away against my will, and Danny rescued me. Quite heroically, as a matter of fact. So you're wasting your time trying to intimidate him. He's been up against far worse than you. I suggest you find something more constructive to do. Danny and I are going home."

We strode forward, and the gang melted before us. Their bewildered faces made me want to laugh, but I restrained myself until we'd passed through the close and into the maze of narrow streets surrounding it. Then I let go with a whoop. Mum joined me.

"You were terrific, Mum!" I threw my arms around her waist.

"And so were you," she replied, tousling my hair. "Now let's go home."

WHEN WE TURNED ONTO OUR OWN street, I saw a figure coming toward us, head down, coat collar turned up against the wind. My heart stood still—no, Dad wasn't stumbling or weaving, just trudging, as if the effort cost him everything he had. I glanced at Mum. She hadn't recognized him yet. She'd never seen him like this, all his raw strength worn down to a brittle shell.

I touched her arm. A pigeon flew up in front of Dad's face and he raised his head, startled. Then his eyes fell on me. First they widened in shock, then kindled in joy, then darkened toward anger as he hurried toward us.

"Where the blazes have you been, boy? You had me worried sick. The police, the cathedral, the whole bloody town out looking for you, and you saunter down the street as bold as brass. I ought to—"

Then he threw his arms around me and squeezed till I gasped for breath. "Oh, Danny, I thought I'd lost you too. Don't ever leave me again, lad. I thought I was done for this time."

I held tight for a minute, then pulled back. "I'm sorry, Dad. I couldn't help it, really. They just took me and I couldn't get back. But see who I've brought with me, Dad. You haven't even looked at her."

Dad pinned me to his side as he turned. "Thank you, ma'am—" He paled and the words died on his lips. "C-Celia? No, it couldn't be . . ."

Mum smiled. "Yes, Michael. It's me."

"Celia . . . I can't believe it. How . . . ? Why . . . ?" I held tight to keep him from toppling over.

"I've been farther away than you can imagine—and I couldn't get back. But Danny came for me. I'm home, Michael. I'm home."

"Celia—" His voice broke. "Then—it wasn't someone else? You didn't leave me?"

"Leave you? My own Michael? Never." Her voice shook as well.

He put out a tentative hand and brushed his fingertips against her cheek. "Celia," he breathed again, as if only saying her name could make her come real.

I stood, knowing I shouldn't be watching but unable to tear my eyes away. From the cathedral the bells began to toll.

Dad blinked as if coming out of a dream. "That's the first bell for Evensong, lad. Service of Lessons and Carols. You'd best get a move on. They'll be wanting you."

So I hadn't missed it after all! The elúndina had brought us back to just a few days after I'd left. I gave my parents a last quick squeeze and dashed back to the cathedral.

All the boys clamored to hear where I'd been, but there was no time to explain. I wriggled into my robe, and Canon Howard, looking faint with relief, just shooed me into place as we did a quick warm-up, then formed into two lines for our entrance. We processed slowly in from the narthex and up either side of the nave, singing.

From the stalls, I scanned the congregation. Mum and Dad sat near the front, with moist eyes and broad smiles.

I stepped out and lifted my voice in my opening solo. "I Wonder as I Wander," I sang—and knew my wandering was at an end.

Author's Note

YOU WILL NOT FIND MIDCHESTER on any map of England. The Midchester cathedral and choir school bear some resemblance to those of Chichester, but as I have not had the privilege of visiting Chichester and have had to take a number of architectural and organizational liberties for the sake of my story, I thought it best to create a fictional town.

P.S. It is unlikely you will find Falenda on any astronomical map either. But if you do, by all means let me know.

A Brief Guide to the Falendan Language

PRONUNCIATION GUIDE

Syllables with an accent mark (´) are stressed. Longer words also have secondary stresses.

Consonants are pronounced as you would expect from English. The "c" is always pronounced as "k." The "g" is always hard, as in "grow."

Vowels are pronounced consistently in the following way:

"a" as in "ah"

"e" as in "met"

"i" like "ee" in "feet"

"o" as in "vote"

"u" like "oo" in "food"

Vocabulary and Names

Balikúni   Creatures one can ride; like a cross between a horse, a camel, a unicorn, and a chameleon

Búrika   Green birdlike creatures that lay tiny fuchsia-speckled eggs

Calivóda   Healing hot springs for bathing or drinking

Carfánu   Storm of flaming rocks

Elífalu   Original name of Hakagrug, then leader of the elúndina

Elúndina   Butterfly-angels, servants of the Great One, who materialize out of light

Falakúr   Meli's father

Garáma   Grey vines that grow on the malacána trees

Hákagrug   Evil being trapped under the mountains who causes City-dwellers to be Flattened

Kalotelaméliku   The Crystal Village—Meli's home village

Lenafálina   Multicolored crystals or gems with various powers. Green = surface healing, red = deep/bone healing, blue = improves eyesight, violet = contains thoughts in a *likúmena*, gold = controls the mind/heals diseases of the mind. Other colors impart skill in various arts, but this does not come into the story.

Lenafálina can be "alive," in which case they exercise their powers, or "dead," in which case they are merely like jewels. The Dome over the City is constructed of dead lenafálina.

Likúmena   Multisensory "book" made of a sheet of violet *lenafálina*

Lódamor   Young man of Telatilamélu, betrothed to Meli by traditional arrangement

Logoságami   Wise man or woman who communicates with

192

the *elúndina* and has other special powers; acts as leader
of a village

Lóravel   Young man of highland village who accompanies
Danny to the City

Lucáfu   Sheep/goat-like creatures, kept for their milk and
their iridescent wool. All Falendan fabrics are made from
lucáfu wool.

Malacána   Orange-colored trees with foliage like giant dandelion clocks

Márala   Meli's mother

Méliku   Crystal

Melikulenduliminála   Meli's full name, meaning "Child of the
Crystal"

Melikunápitu   Nourishing drink that flows from the crystal

Misamárila   Sin or offense

Níkhi   Moth-demons, servants of Hakagrug that materialize out of darkness and plant evil thoughts in people's
minds

Níla   Meli's balikuni mare

Nousíniki   Falendan "hair," defined as "that which knows the
spirit." Gives Falendans power to communicate telepath-
ically; lights up in the darkness; gives buoyancy when
climbing or running; senses danger.

Pantelèia   A healing herb

Ruávena   Wife of *Tulamen*

Telamalacánu   The Village of the Trees, where Danny and
Meli hope to lodge but are driven off by nikhi

Telatilamélu   The Village within the Vines, where Danny and
Meli spend the first night of their journey

Tílamel   Deep-blue vines that offer protection from nikhi and
evil air

Tower of Grózlukh   Tall tower in the middle of the City; Enemy stronghold

Túlamen   Highland cottager who accompanies Danny to the City

Váli   Danny's balikuni stallion

About the Author

KATHERINE BOLGER HYDE TAUGHT HERSELF to read at age four and has rarely been without a book since. Katherine writes the Crime with the Classics traditional mystery series for adults as well as fantasy and picture books for children. She lives in California with her husband and two obstreperous cats. In her spare time she can usually be found knitting while watching British mystery shows or singing soprano in the choir at St. Lawrence Orthodox Church.

OTHER BOOKS BY KATHERINE BOLGER HYDE

PICTURE BOOKS
Lucia, Saint of Light (Ancient Faith Publishing, 2009)
Everything Tells Us about God (Ancient Faith Publishing, 2018)

CRIME WITH THE CLASSICS
Arsenic with Austen (Minotaur, 2016)
Bloodstains with Brontë (Minotaur, 2017)
Cyanide with Christie (Severn House, 2019)
Death with Dostoevsky (Severn House, 2019)

CPSIA information can be obtained
at www.ICGtesting.com
Printed in the USA
JSHW030508140121
10919JS00003B/16

9 781732 087323